"No[...]"

"Of cou[...] [...]epped back. "I'm sorry, Travis. [...] right. I should never have…"

He hauled her into his arms again. He kissed her over and over, until she was clinging to him. "Don't ever apologize for wanting me. Don't you know how exciting that is, Princess? To know you feel the way I feel? I have a suite at the inn. It's where I planned on spending the night. Will you come there with me, and let me make love to you as if this were our first time?"

He waited for her answer, knowing that giving her time to think was a gamble. He was asking her to admit her need for him, instead of being swept away by it, but he didn't want her to come to him blinded by passion. Not tonight. Tonight he wanted to seduce her. Awaken her. And to know, after this, the only man she would remember would be him.

"Alex." He ran his thumb over her parted lips. "I want to make love to you. Tell me it's what you want, too."

His answer was in the soft surrender of her kiss.

THE BARONS

**Four brothers:
bonded by inheritance, battling for love!**

Jonas Baron is approaching his eighty-fifth
birthday. He has ruled Espada, his sprawling
estate in Texas hill country, for more than
forty years, but now he admits it's time he
chose an heir.

Jonas has three sons—Gage, Travis and Slade,
all ruggedly handsome and each with a successful
business empire of his own; none wishes to give
up the life he's fought for to take over Espada.
Jonas also has a stepdaughter; beautiful and
spirited, Caitlin loves the land as much as he
does, but she's not of the Baron blood.

So who will receive Baron's bequest? As Gage,
Travis, Slade and Caitlin discover, there's more at
stake than just Espada. For love also has its part
to play in deciding their futures....

Sit back now and enjoy Travis's story, and be
sure to look out next for **Slade Baron's Bride** in
November (Harlequin Presents® #2063), when
you'll get to know Slade a whole lot better!

SANDRA MARTON

More Than a Mistress

THE BARONS

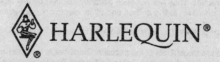

HARLEQUIN®

TORONTO • NEW YORK • LONDON
AMSTERDAM • PARIS • SYDNEY • HAMBURG
STOCKHOLM • ATHENS • TOKYO • MILAN • MADRID
PRAGUE • WARSAW • BUDAPEST • AUCKLAND

ISBN 0-373-12045-1

MORE THAN A MISTRESS

First North American Publication 1999.

Copyright © 1999 by Sandra Marton.

All rights reserved. Except for use in any review, the reproduction or utilization of this work in whole or in part in any form by any electronic, mechanical or other means, now known or hereafter invented, including xerography, photocopying and recording, or in any information storage or retrieval system, is forbidden without the written permission of the publisher, Harlequin Enterprises Limited, 225 Duncan Mill Road, Don Mills, Ontario, Canada M3B 3K9.

All characters in this book have no existence outside the imagination of the author and have no relation whatsoever to anyone bearing the same name or names. They are not even distantly inspired by any individual known or unknown to the author, and all incidents are pure invention.

This edition published by arrangement with Harlequin Books S.A.

® and TM are trademarks of the publisher. Trademarks indicated with ® are registered in the United States Patent and Trademark Office, the Canadian Trade Marks Office and in other countries.

Look us up on-line at: http://www.romance.net

Printed in U.S.A.

CHAPTER ONE

TRAVIS BARON stood in the wings of the improvised stage at the Hotel Paradise, a hint of defiance in the rake of his jaw, waiting to be auctioned off to the highest bidder.

And wasn't that a hell of a thing for a man to be doing on a beautiful Thursday night in early June? Travis thought grimly.

He ran his fingers through his hair, then smoothed his hand down the lapel of his tux. He couldn't see the crowd in the elegant ballroom but he could damn well hear it, every feminine hoot, whistle and catcall. This was the crème de la crème of L.A. society, Pete Haskell had said. Maybe so. But they sure sounded pretty down-and-dirty from where Travis stood.

The wheedling drone of the auctioneer's voice oozed from the loudspeakers like honey from a comb on a hot Texas day.

"What'm-I-bid, what'm-I-bid, ladies, c'mon, c'mon, don't be shy, don't hold back. Win the man of your dreams for the weekend."

Shy? Travis snorted. Based on what he'd been hearing for the past hour, the women gathered in the ballroom were about as shy as a herd of buffalo, and about as delicate in making their wants known. They cheered, they laughed, they hooted and hollered until the gavel came down and then they applauded and whistled until Travis figured the noise level was enough to have the riot cops bust the place. And then they started up all over again, when the next hapless victim was shoved out on stage.

Not that all the Bachelors for Bucks had to be pushed.

Lots of them went willingly, grinning and throwing kisses to the crowd.

"Hey, man," one guy had said, after a look at Travis's glum expression, "it's all for charity, right?"

Right, Travis thought, his scowl darkening. But the guy with the smile had probably volunteered for this nonsense. Travis hadn't. And to make things even worse, the luck of the draw was sending him out on that stage last.

How, he thought, *how* had he let himself get talked into this mess?

"Sold!" The auctioneer's triumphant shout and the smack of his gavel were drowned out in a burst of cheers and applause.

"Another one gone," a voice mumbled, and Travis turned as a skinny blond guy stepped up beside him, his Adam's apple bobbing as he adjusted his tie. "Man, I'd rather be going for a root canal."

"You got that right," Travis said.

"Now, now, gentlemen." Peggy Jeffers, who'd cheerfully introduced herself as "your friendly slave mistress for the evening" when they'd all been introduced, tweaked the skinny guy's cheek. "You just relax, go on out there and have yourself some fun."

"Fun?" the guy said, "Fun?"

"Fun," Peggy repeated, and she put her hand in the middle of his back and gently pushed him out of the wings and onto the stage.

The roar of the audience sent the blood right to Travis's head.

Peggy smiled. "Hear that?"

"Yeah," Travis said, with what he hoped would pass for a smile. "Sounds like a pack of hyenas on a blood trail."

Peggy giggled. "You got that right." She took a step back, then eyeballed Travis from the top of his sun-streaked chestnut hair to the toes of his shiny black boots. "My oh my, handsome. They're gonna go nuts when they spot you."

She grinned, and Travis tried to return it.

"Don't tell me a hunk like you is nervous," Peggy said.

"No," Travis said, lying through his teeth. "Why would I be nervous about going out on that stage in front of a million screaming women to get myself auctioned off?"

Peggy laughed. "It's all for a good cause," she said over her shoulder as she hurried away. "And you'll get snapped up in a second."

Yeah, Travis thought, oh, yeah. That's what he'd been telling himself all night—that, and the fact that he was a sane man, a normal, healthy, sane, thirty-two-year-old attorney. A bachelor, yes...but a bachelor who liked to choose his own women.

And choose them, he did. All the time. If he had any problems with women, it was getting them to understand, when the moment of truth came, that all good things came to an end. Relationships between the sexes weren't meant to last forever. A bad marriage and a worse divorce had finally taught him what the lessons of his childhood hadn't, but those two blips in the road were long behind him.

It wasn't as if he was opposed to women coming on to him. He liked a little aggressiveness in a woman, in bed and out. He found it sexy.

But a woman hitting on a guy she spotted at a party was one thing. Bidding for him, as if he were a slab of meat...

That was something else.

He'd been conned. And it had happened during a partners meeting at Sullivan, Cohen and Vittali a few months ago.

If only he'd realized that Pete Haskell was setting him up.

"Hey, Baron," Pete had said casually, as he bit into a bagel, "I was talking about you the other day with some guys from Hannan and Murphy."

"Ah," Travis had said, with a smile, "were they telling you how much they wish I'd accepted a partnership there instead of here?"

Pete chuckled. "Actually, we were talking about the

Bachelors for Bucks thing. You know, the annual charity auction?''

"That's still going on?"

"Yup." Pete buttered the other half of his bagel. "They're figuring the new guy they hired is gonna come in at an all-time high bid."

"No way," one of the other partners said.

Pete shrugged. "They're taking bets he will, John. They figure nobody can beat him, considering his record."

"What record?" John reached for the sweetener. "The guy talks too much, you know what I mean? Any man blabs endlessly about all the broads in his life, well, right away, I have my doubts. No man has that much time, much less stamina." John grinned. "Well, except for ol' Travis, here."

Pete nodded thoughtfully. "I agree." He shot Travis a look. "But Travis never talks. Never lets us in on what he's been doing, and who and how often he's been doing it with."

Travis looked up from his coffee and grinned. "I am a man of honor," he said. "I never talk about my women." His grin broadened. "And the silence just kills you, pal, doesn't it?"

"But," Pete said, undeterred, "we all know what a stud our Travis is. Talk about his latest conquest is a staple in the secretaries' lunchroom. We spot the newest lady getting out of a taxi in front of the building at quitting time." He grinned. "And we watch the bouquets of long-stemmed roses fly out of the florist's shop next door, when Trav decides it's time to dump a broad."

"Please," Travis said, his hand to his heart. "I'd never send roses. Everybody sends roses."

"So, what do you send?"

The partners all looked up from their coffee. Old man Sullivan was the one who'd asked the question. It was the first time he'd said a word during a meeting in six months.

"Whatever flowers seem appropriate for that particular

lady,'' Travis said, and smiled. ''And something small but tasteful, with a note that says—''

''Thanks, but no thanks,'' Sullivan suggested, and everyone laughed.

''The thing is,'' Pete said, ''I told the guys from Hannan and Murphy that they could boast all they like about their man getting the high bid, considering that our man didn't even enter.''

''Which he hadn't, and isn't,'' Travis said firmly.

''Oh, I know that. We all know that. Right, boys?''

Later, Travis would remember that everybody in the room, even the two female partners, nodded vigorously, then put their heads down as if on cue. But right at that moment, Pete's comments had seemed casual.

''And they said?''

Pete sighed. ''They said that we're all lawyers, and we should know better than to present a case with nothing but hearsay evidence.''

Someone groaned. Someone else laughed, but old man Sullivan narrowed his rheumy eyes and leaned forward in his chair at the head of the boardroom table.

''And, Peter?''

''And,'' Pete said, after a barely perceptible pause, ''they challenged us. They said we should put our boy, Travis, on the block.''

''No way,'' Travis said quickly.

''Then, they said, we'll really see which guy wins.'' He paused dramatically. ''And the firm that loses has to treat the other to a golf weekend at Pebble Beach.''

''Cool,'' somebody said, and then a wild cheer went up around the walnut-paneled room.

''Now, wait just a minute,'' Travis had started to say, but old man Sullivan was already smiling across the table and assuring Travis that they all knew he'd carry their banner high into battle, and make them proud to be partners in Sullivan, Cohen and Vittali.

Trapped, Travis thought grimly. It had been a conspiracy.

Old man Sullivan had probably been the only one not in on the scheme. Not that it mattered. There'd been no way out of the setup, not without hearing about it forever from the rest of the partners. And so now here he was, a man about to go onstage before a crowd of estrogen-crazed females like a lamb being led to the slaughter, and if he came in at a penny lower than five grand—which was what Hannan and Murphy's entry had gone for—he'd never live it down.

"I didn't really have a choice," he'd said to his kid brother, over the phone. "Anyway, it's for a good cause. All the money raised goes to children's hospitals."

"Sure," Slade had said, and then he'd snorted.

"What?"

"Well, I was just thinkin'…" Slade's voice took on the soft, Texas drawl of their childhood. "It's kind of like a bull bein' auctioned off to a herd of heifers."

"It's a legitimate auction," Travis had said coldly, and slammed down the phone. Then he'd picked it up, punched in the code for Slade's Boston number again and said, before Slade could say a word, that he should have known better than to have expected sympathy from his own flesh and blood.

"You got it, bro," Slade had replied, and laughed until, at last, Travis had laughed, too, and said how bad would it really be…

Travis shuddered. "Bad," he whispered, and closed his eyes.

All the senior partners and associates were in the audience. The clerks and the secretaries were waiting by their telephones, eager to hear how their entry did because this thing had taken on a life of its own, with side bets, pool bets…

How much would he go for? Would he top the Hannan and Murphy guy? Where would he place in the overall standings? Would the woman who "bought" him be good-looking? A ten, on the nutty scale the secretaries had drawn up? A five? Or, as his own secretary had explained, with a shudder, would a two or even a one be the winner?

Travis groaned.

Unless he went for the right price, to the right female, he'd never live it down. And there was just no way to tell how things would go, once he got on stage and put his fate in the hands of the auctioneer and the wild-women masquerading as solid citizens. Why hadn't he had the brains to set things up? Bought a ticket for Sally—no, not Sally. He'd just sent her a bouquet of dog-toothed violets and an eight ounce bottle of Chanel. Okay, then. Bethany. He could have bought Bethany a ticket, told her to bid a thousand bucks more than whatever the Hannan and Murphy guy went for and he'd pay her back—with interest.

Except, what good was a bet, if you had to cheat to win it?

There was no choice except to leave the bidding up to fate. And he, of all people, knew that fate wasn't always kind, not even for an event as silly as this.

"Your turn next, Cowboy."

Travis jerked upright at the sound of Peggy's voice.

"Great," he said stiffly. "The sooner we get this over with, the better."

"Want me to take a peek at the house? Tell you who hasn't bought herself a hunk yet and looks as if she might be willing to pay a decent price for you?"

"It's unimportant," he said, with dignity, and she laughed.

"Move over, and let me look."

"Look? Look where?"

"There's a tiny crack, right here..." Peggy slipped up beside him and put her eye to the wall. "Aha!"

"Aha, what?" Travis asked, despite his best intentions to appear disinterested.

"There are definitely some—what do you guys call them now? Foxes? Babes?"

"Attractive women," Travis said with dignity, and sent up a silent thank-you.

"Yeah, I'll bet. Okay, then, handsome, there are some attractive women." She sighed. "And some so-so's."

"Well," Travis said valiantly, "that's fine."

"And…" Peggy stiffened. "Uh-oh."

Travis froze. "Uh-oh, what?"

"Uh-oh, there's a lady right in the center who, uh, who probably has a great personality. A terrific personality, you might say."

"I'm sure she has," Travis said bravely.

"And I'm sure the woman with the feather boa and the rhinestone tiara at the table right behind her will fascinate you no end."

"Oh." His shoulders slumped. "As bad as that?"

"And then there's the blue-eyed blonde who just walked in. Oh, I hate her on sight! Great hair. Great face. Great bod, from what I can see of it. Mark my words, Cowboy. Any woman who looks like that probably has the intellect of a potato."

Travis laughed. "Meow."

"I'm just being honest. You get looks like that and, to compensate, you get empty space between your ears. And the disposition of a weasel."

"A weasel, huh?" Travis grinned. "Whoever said women were the gentle sex didn't know what he was talking about."

"Well, it's the truth." Peggy stepped closer, smoothed down his lapels. "So you do yourself a favor, Cowboy. Go on out there and play to the crowd. To the—what'd you call 'em?—the 'attractive women.' Heck, if you're feeling generous, maybe even to the, uh, the lady with the terrific personality." She smiled. "Forget about the Ice Princess."

Travis smiled, too. Suddenly, with the moment of truth upon him, he saw all his worries for the foolishness they were. And he owed the revelation to Peggy.

He took her hand and bowed over it.

"Ah, Slave Mistress, you have my heartfelt gratitude. To hell with Pebble Beach and my reputation."

"Huh?"

"Never mind." He lifted her fingers to his lips. "Too bad you're not out there bidding, m'love. I'd be honored to be yours for the weekend."

Peggy blushed furiously and pulled her fingers free of his just as the gavel sounded and the crowd roared.

"You'll do lots better than me," she said, and gently shoved him toward the stage. "Go on, handsome. Get out there and knock 'em dead."

Which was exactly what Travis decided he'd do.

He went onstage at a brisk trot, arms high overhead, hands clasped in a winner's pose, and did a fair imitation of Sylvester Stallone's victory dance in *Rocky,* while flashing a thousand-watt grin.

The crowd loved it, and roared its approval.

Travis laughed. What he'd told Peggy was the truth. This wasn't real life. It was for a good cause. And it was fun, or it was supposed to be. If the jerks in his office had made it into something else, that was their problem, not his.

So what if he went for five hundred bucks? So what if he wasn't snapped up by a hot-looking babe? Let everybody at Sullivan, Cohen and Vittali have a laugh at his expense. Let 'em lose their crazy bets. He was going to get into the spirit of things, have some fun and do his best to raise a bundle of bucks for kids who really needed—

Uh-oh.

Travis's smile dimmed just a little as he spotted the lady at the center table nearest the stage. Peggy had certainly nailed it right. The lady was certain to have a great personality. Well, so what? She had a nice smile. Hey, she was probably a nice person. The auctioneer was doing his intro, a bit about Travis Baron, Esquire, and Travis strutted a little more, grinned when somebody let out a piercing wolf whistle and shot a big smile to the lady in the front.

"Do I hear five hundred dollars to start?" the auctioneer

said, and the lady with the smile and the personality whooped and said, "How about a thousand?"

A cheer went up and Travis smiled, and looked at her, looked past her...

And thought, just for a second, that his heart was going to leap straight out of his chest.

A woman was standing behind the last tables. He knew, right away, she was the latecomer Peggy had described.

She was also the most beautiful woman Travis had ever seen in his life.

Peggy had said she was blonde and blue-eyed. With great hair, a great face and a great body.

All correct. And all wrong, because those words didn't come anywhere close to describing her.

Her hair was a cascade of silk the color of ripening wheat, her eyes the color of Texas bluebells. Her face was a perfect oval, with those incredible blue eyes darkly lashed and wide-set under slender, arched brows. She had a proud, straight nose, a sexy indentation above her mouth...

Oh, that mouth. The full upper lip. The softly curved lower one.

It was a mouth made for kissing.

His gaze dropped lower, to the tanned shoulders left bare by a halter-necked dress the color of garnets, to the generous lift of her breasts, the slender waist and rounded hips. Her skirt ended at midthigh, revealing a long length of shapely leg.

His blood hummed in his ears.

He wanted her. Wanted her with a primal need and desire that surpassed anything he'd ever known. He wanted to kiss that mouth, caress that body...and melt the coldness that clung to her like an invisible sheath of ice. He could see it in her posture. In the way she didn't so much as blink when his eyes met hers again. In the defiant lift of her chin.

He knew she could see the frank, sexual appraisal in his gaze—and that it didn't matter a damn to her.

Look all you like, she seemed to say, but don't be foolish enough to think you can have what you see.

Travis felt his body tighten. The sounds of the cheering women, the drone of the auctioneer, faded to a dull roar.

He imagined himself coming down off that stage. Going to her. Taking her in his arms. No words. No niceties. Just taking her in his arms, carrying her out of the ballroom to a place where they'd be alone, ripping that piece of dark red silk from her body and burying himself deep inside her while she wrapped her arms and legs around him...

Oh, hell.

He was standing in front of hundreds of people, thinking things that could only bring a man public humiliation. Stop it, he told himself fiercely, and he tore his gaze from her, thought about cold showers and forced himself to focus on the delighted faces of the crowd.

"I have five thousand," the auctioneer shouted. "Do I hear six?"

"Six," the lady in the front yelled.

Travis fixed his attention on her. He flashed a sexy smile. She squealed. He turned his back to the audience, looked over his shoulder and pretended he was going to slip his jacket off.

The crowd whooped and cheered.

"Six-five," a brunette shouted. Travis turned and blew her a kiss.

He didn't need the blonde Ice Princess. He had a trio of women in a frenzied bidding war over him. What more could a guy ask?

"Seven," a stunning redhead said.

"Hey," he shouted, "I'm worth a lot more than that!"

The crowd stamped its well-shod feet in approval. The brunette laughed, and another redhead shot to her feet. "Seven-five," she called, and everybody cheered and applauded.

Travis grinned. The guy from Hannan and Murphy had gone for five.

"I'm worth more than that, too," he yelled.

The crowd loved it.

"Eight," the lady in the front said.

"Eight-five," the brunette shouted.

"Nine!"

Travis laughed. The evening he'd dreaded was turning out to be fun. One more glance at the blonde, that was all, before the gavel swung down. Not that it mattered. He'd probably overestimated her looks. If she'd walked farther into the room so that she was closer to the stage, he'd have seen her flaws.

What flaws?

She *had* come closer, while the bidding was raging. She was almost at the stage and Lord, she wasn't beautiful, she was spectacular.

And she was looking at him. Her expression was difficult to read. Interested, yes, but it seemed...

Speculative. As if she were appraising him. And finding him wanting.

Travis's hands knotted at his sides as the woman turned swiftly and started back up the aisle.

Who did this babe think she was, to check him out and then walk away? Turn around, he thought furiously, turn around!

The woman's pace increased.

Travis took a step forward. To hell with the auction!

"Nine thousand," the auctioneer shouted, and the crowd roared. "Nine thousand once. Nine thousand twice..."

"Ten," the brunette screamed.

The blonde woman stopped. That's it, baby, Travis thought. Turn around. Look at me.

And she did. Her eyes met his. Their gazes locked, and held. For one breathless moment, there was no one else in the room, no one else in the universe. It was only them. Travis, and the woman.

She knew it, too.

He saw her acknowledge it as her eyes widened, saw the

impact of the understanding in the sudden, rapid rise and
fall of her breasts. The tip of her tongue—a pale, silken
pink—slipped over her soft-looking mouth.

Travis's eyes bored into hers. Do it, he thought. Do it, do
it...

"Going once," the auctioneer said, "to the lady at table
three, for ten thousand dollars. Going twice. Going—"

"Twenty thousand dollars."

The crowd gasped. Every head swiveled toward the
woman with the blond hair. Even the auctioneer leaned forward.

"Would you repeat your bid, please, madam?"

The woman took a deep breath. Travis thought he saw
her tremble but he knew he must have been mistaken, because when she spoke again, her voice was cool, controlled,
and touched with something that bordered on amusement.

"I said, I bid twenty thousand dollars."

Bang went the gavel. "Sold," the auctioneer said, tri-
umphantly, "to the lady in red."

And the crowd in the ballroom of the Hotel Paradise
went wild.

CHAPTER TWO

THE bang of the gavel echoed through the ballroom, but it wasn't as loud as the sudden thump of Alexandra Thorpe's heart.

"Sold," the auctioneer shouted. "Sold to the lady in red."

The lady in red, she thought numbly...

Alex thought, for an instant, her legs would buckle. She bowed her head and gripped the chair in front of her. She'd come here to buy a man, and she had. A man named Travis Baron.

A stud named Travis Baron, a little voice inside her said coldly. It was true. The man onstage was every inch a stud, if looks and attitude were anything to go by...

And now, she owned him.

Why on earth had she done something so stupid? Carl's words had hurt, yes, but so what? Their divorce was two years old. She didn't miss Carl, or love him; she knew now that she never really had. So, why should anything he said, *anything,* still haunt her? And the rest of her plan, if you could call it that, was not just stupid but sick. A woman didn't just—a woman couldn't just—

Awareness sizzled thought her blood.

He was looking at her. Every nerve ending in her body was screaming it.

Don't, Alex told herself, don't lift your head....

Stopping the rotation of the planet would have been easier. Alex caught her bottom lip between her teeth and slowly raised her eyes to the stage.

Her heart did it again, just as it had when he'd first looked at her. It took that leap within her breast that made the room spin. Travis Baron hadn't moved. Those hot green eyes were still fixed on her as if he was a hawk and she was his prey. There was a smile of pure masculine satisfaction, tilting across his mouth—that sensual mouth—she could almost feel on her own. Everything about him, from the set of his broad shoulders, the way he stood, with his long legs planted slightly apart, sent a message, and the message was unmistakable.

I am a man, he was saying. And you are a woman. And when you and I are alone…

Panic whispered along Alex's skin. She would *never* be alone with this man, or with any other. She had learned that much from her marriage. Forgetting that lesson, tonight, had been an aberration, a foolish reaction to an overheard whisper that had called back painful memories.

What did she give a damn, if Carl had told his new wife she was frigid? Let him say what he liked, so long as he was no longer saying it to her.

Alex tore her gaze from Travis Baron's. People were crowding around her, offering congratulations.

"What will you do with that gorgeous hunk for an entire weekend?" a woman said, and a roar of laughter went up.

She knew it was only a joke. The auction was a legitimate fund-raiser. What the winners did with their bachelors was play tennis, or golf, go dancing or to dinner…

Except, that wasn't what she'd intended to do with him.

The thought was enough to send another wave of panic rolling through her blood. Alex smiled. She hoped she smiled, anyway, and laughed, and said she'd think of something…

With the laughter still ringing in her ears, she fled up the aisle toward the double doors that led to the lobby, and to sanity.

"Mrs. Stuart?"

Just keep walking, Alex. Smile, and keep…

"Mrs. Stuart." A hand clasped her arm.

Alex shook off the hand. "No," she said…and looked into the puzzled face of a gray-haired woman.

"I'm terribly sorry, Mrs. Stuart. I didn't mean to startle you."

Alex swallowed, pulled her lips into another parody of a smile. "I'm sorry. I don't—"

The woman smiled, too, and looped her arm through Alex's. "We've met before, Mrs. Stuart. Perhaps you'll recall? I'm Barbara Rhodes. Our husbands served on the water conservation committee together."

"My ex-husband," Alex said. "I use my maiden name. I'm Alexandra Thorpe now."

The woman winced. "Yes, of course. Sorry. I'd forgotten."

"That's quite all right. Now, if you'll excuse me..."

"Oh, I know you're in a hurry to pay for your purchase."

"My purchase," Alex said, and felt the color shoot into her face.

"Yes. We've set up a desk, in the lobby." The woman led Alex toward the double doors. "But I wanted to take a moment to thank you, personally, for making tonight's high bid."

"Ah." Alex smiled again and wondered if it were possible for your lips to stick to your teeth. "No need," she said brightly. "I'm more than happy to—help out."

"If only everyone felt that way. But let me tell you, Ms. Thorpe, they don't. As chairperson of the auction these last two years, I know how rarely people make such generous donations."

"Yes." Someone batted the doors open and Alex and the chairperson stepped through them. "Well, I know—I know what fine work your organization does, Mrs. Rhodes..."

"Have you decided what you'll do with your bachelor, Ms. Thorpe?"

Alex swallowed dryly. "No. No, I... Actually, I doubt if I'll, ah, if I'll use him at all, Mrs. Rhodes. I, uh, I already have plans for the weekend."

"Oh, that's too bad."

"Yes, it is, isn't it?" Alex came to a stop, opened her beaded purse and dug inside it. "Look, why don't we do this right now? I'll make out a check, give it to you—"

"Well, you're supposed to pay at the desk... Oh, never mind. I'm happy to make an accommodation for you."

Alex took out her checkbook. "The Children's Hospital Fund, right?" Her hands were trembling. Could she write out the check and sign it so it was legible? She scrawled the name of the fund and the amount she'd bid—the incredible amount she'd bid, for a man she could only pray she'd never see again—signed her name, ripped out the check and handed it to the chairwoman, who beamed happily and clutched it to her ample breasts.

"Wonderful, Ms. Thorpe. And now..."

"And now," Alex said with false gaiety, "I'll just be on my way."

"Certainly. But first, if we could just prevail upon you to stay for a few pictures, while you dance with Mr. Baron. For publicity purposes, you understand."

Alex shook her head. "No! I mean, I just explained, I have plans..."

"For the weekend. Yes, but this will only take a few minutes." The woman took Alex's arm. "Do you know anything about him?"

"Not a thing," Alex said briskly.

"Oh, he's a fascinating man. So handsome! And those cowboy boots..." The chairwoman sighed. "Oh, if I were only twenty years younger. Unmarried. Well, and forty pounds lighter..."

She laughed gaily, and Alex tried to do the same.

"It will only take a minute, Ms. Thorpe." She beamed a happy smile in Alex's direction. "The TV people are here. If you and your bachelor could give them a few pictures. And a short interview? It would be wonderful publicity for the auction."

"He's not 'my' bachelor," Alex said, rushing the words together. "You don't understand, Mrs. Rhodes. I've no time to do any of this. Really, I can't..."

"But you can, Ms. Thorpe," a deep voice said. "And you will."

Alex froze. The tempo of her heartbeat increased to something a rock-and-roll drummer would have envied. She took a quick step back and knew, too late, that she'd made yet another mistake because stepping back brought her into contact with the hard, male body that belonged to the voice.

Barbara Rhodes's eyebrows flew toward her hairline, and Alex knew her fear must have shown in her face. So she took a deep breath, gave a wobbly smile and said, "Oh, dear, I can see that I'm trapped." And then, still smiling, still feeling the race of her pulse in her throat, she turned and looked up into the face of Travis Baron.

"Hello, Sugar," he said softly, and smiled.

Onstage, he'd looked handsome and masculine. But up close—up close...

Alex's heartbeat ratcheted up another notch.

Up close, he was spectacular.

Tall. Tall enough so even she, at five-eight in her stocking feet, had to tilt her head back to look up to him, and she'd worn ridiculously high heels tonight, to go with the equally ridiculous dress. Tall, and gorgeous, with those hot eyes. And a nose that surely had once been broken. And that mouth. That sexy, almost cruel mouth.

Mrs. Rhodes was right. The man she'd won was handsome. He was gorgeous. He was the fulfillment of every wild, middle-of-the-night dream she'd ever had, in the long-ago days when she'd still been foolish enough to dream.

And he was dangerous. Even she could tell that.

What were you thinking tonight, Alexandra?

The chairwoman looked from Alex to Travis, and then she let out a girlish laugh. "Well. I can see I'm not needed anymore."

"No," Travis said bluntly, his eyes never leaving Alexandra Thorpe's. "No, you're not."

"My." Mrs. Rhodes fanned her face with Alex's check. "My, oh my. Uh, thank you again, Mrs....Ms. Thorpe. And thank you, too, Mr. Baron. If you need anything, anything at all..."

Travis reached out, took Alex's arm and drew her away from the chairwoman.

"Which is it?" he said.

Alex blinked. "I—I beg your pardon?"

"She called you Mrs. Then she called you Ms."

His hand tightened on her arm. Alex looked down, saw the darkness of his fingers against the paleness of her skin. And forced herself to take a deep, deep breath.

"It's…" *Lie. Tell him you're married. Tell him anything. Just get away. Get away, while you can…* "It's…" Her eyes met his. "If I said it was Mrs. would you go away?"

He smiled. The smile made his mouth tilt and his eyes get even darker. Most of all, it made her stomach drop toward her toes.

"Not until you introduced me to your husband, so I could see for myself what kind of man would be stupid enough to leave a woman like you so unsatisfied that she'd look at a stranger with so much hunger."

Color flooded Alex's cheeks. "Mr. Baron—"

"Are you married, or aren't you?"

"I'm divorced. And if you think I looked—that I looked…"

"I don't think, Sugar. I know."

Travis slid his hand down her arm, to her wrist. He'd thought of all the things he'd say to this woman as he'd battled his way through the crowd toward her. Subtle things. Soft things. How beautiful she was. What he'd felt at the sight of her. But standing close to her, with the scent of her in his nostrils and the silken feel of her skin under his fingertips, he'd suddenly known that there was no reason to be subtle, or cautious. He was on fire, and so was she, and he'd be damned if he'd play games.

"You need me," he said, very softly. "And I need you. And I promise you, we'll satisfy our needs before this night ends."

His words should have shocked her. Instead, they excited her. Alex felt her body turning molten with heat. His voice was like warm, heavy cream, pouring over her, through her. She looked into those deep green eyes and thought, yes, he could do that for me, he could…

Alex, the little voice within her said sharply, *whatever are you thinking?*

Carefully, politely, she disengaged her hand from his.

"I'm sure that line works wonderfully wherever it is you come from, Mr. Baron."

Travis's eyes narrowed. "Is that what you think that was?"

"And an interesting one, I must admit." Generations of good breeding, coupled with four years as Carl Stuart's wife, made it possible to offer a cool smile. "But I'm afraid you've misread the situation."

"You're lying," he said bluntly.

Alex gave a trilling laugh. "I'll try not to take offense at that, Mr. Baron. Perhaps such comments are acceptable, in your part of the world."

"That's the second time you've made that reference." Travis folded his arms and rocked back on his boot heels. "Is that the problem here? That you're figuring me for a cowboy, and ladies like you don't sleep with the hired help?"

Alex flushed. "If you're trying to be obnoxious, Mr. Baron, let me assure you, you're succeeding."

"I'm being honest, Ms. Thorpe. Which is more than you're doing."

"Mr. Baron. I am, truly, sorry if you've misunderstood the purpose of the auction. It's a charitable event. And I support a great many charities. I've already given the chairwoman my check. And now I've had the—" she paused, almost imperceptibly "—the pleasure of meeting you, sir."

His eyes narrowed. Later, she'd remember that and realize it had been a warning. But right then, analytical thinking was beyond her. All she could think of was escape.

"What you're sayin', Ms. Thorpe, is that you're givin' me the brush-off."

His voice had softened, picked up the faintest drawl. Well, that explained a lot. Cowboy, ranch hand, whatever. She'd missed the description of him, and she hadn't seen the auction catalog, but it didn't matter. She'd figured him right. He wasn't from around here. The auction committee had probably recruited him from a modeling agency, or maybe from Actors' Equity. Los Angeles was filled with men like him, men who'd come here with dreams of stardom.

Wherever he came from, he was accustomed to a macho swagger. It might help him make the cover of *GQ*. It would probably gain him admittance to a lot of L.A. bedrooms, but—

But not hers.

Her behavior back in the ballroom, all that thunder and lightning that had seemed to flash between them, had been the result of remembering how Carl had humiliated her. How even now, with him out of her life, he could still humiliate and infuriate her. Even hurt her.

It had nothing to do with Travis Baron, who was too handsome for his own good, and too untamed for hers.

"Am I right, Ms. Thorpe? Am I gettin' the old heave-ho?"

Alex tilted her head and looked at him with polite interest. A cowboy, and with a dented ego.

Ah, how quickly things had changed.

This was her turf, not his. Too bad he'd learn it the hard way. Too bad she'd come close to forgetting it. She was Alex Thorpe. Buying a man, indeed. Thinking she'd take him to her bed, and for what? To prove something to an ex-husband she didn't give a damn about? She had nothing to prove to anyone, certainly not to herself.

All right, so she'd come rushing to the auction in a mood that was foolish and potentially dangerous. And yes, she'd done a dumb thing, making that bid. But she'd almost done something even more foolish, fleeing. People would talk about her bid for days. Weeks, maybe, until some better bit of gossip came along. Did she want them to also talk about the way she'd run out of the hotel?

She knew what she had to do.

Play out the game. Coolly, with sophistication. A touch of wry humor would be nice. Make it obvious that she'd bid on this man for fun, that she'd done it because she'd wanted to do it, not because of anything more personal.

And not because of the way she'd suddenly felt—suddenly imagined she'd felt—when Travis Baron's eyes had met hers.

The ballroom had emptied out. Those people who'd attended the auction were standing around the lobby in little knots, shooting glances at the two of them with barely concealed interest.

Well, she'd give them something to watch, but not something to remember.

Alex looked up. The cowboy hadn't taken his eyes off her. His expression was still intent. Beyond that, she couldn't read him at all. That troubled her a little, but not much. The balance of power had shifted. She had the upper hand now, and if there was one thing she knew how to do, it was how to use power.

"I'm not giving you the brush-off, Mr. Baron." She lifted her arm, her brows drawing together as she glanced at the tiny gold-and-diamond watch on her wrist. "I do have another appointment. But—"

"Break it."

She laughed gaily, as if he'd made a joke. "Oh, I can't possibly do that. But I do understand my obligations." Still smiling, she lay her hand lightly on his arm. "If you'd be good enough to lead the way into the room that's been set aside for the after-auction party, I'll give you one dance."

"Give it to me?" he said, very softly.

She heard the edge in those simple words and felt the muscles in his arm bunch beneath her fingers. But she was still riding the heady rush that came of knowing both her feet were back on solid ground, and she heard what he said as she wanted to, as an affirmation of which of them had taken control.

"That's right. Perhaps I'll even permit a quick interview." The sound of music drifted from a nearby doorway and she raised her voice, just a little, to be heard over it. "And then, of course, I'll be on my way. You do understand, don't you?"

Oh, yeah, Travis thought, he understood, all right. The Ice Princess had asked him to escort her to the party but it was only a formality. It had been an exercise of privilege and power; how could a man who'd grown up surrounded by such things not recognize it? She was in charge here; the arrogant smile on her face said as much. Without waiting for his reply, she turned and made her way toward the music, confident that he would follow.

A muscle bunched in his jaw. Alexandra Thorpe figured she was playing him for a fool, playing Lady of the Manor to his Bumbling Cowboy. It made him angry as hell, but he wasn't about to let her know that.

Not yet.

He set off after her, as if he'd accepted the part she'd given him.

None of what was happening surprised him. He'd known something was up, after she'd made the winning bid. He'd seen the look on her lovely face go from wanton desire to disbelief. When she'd turned to flee, he'd started to go after her but the other bachelors had rushed on stage to congratulate him and make jokes at his expense. He'd tried to break free but when he saw Barbara Rhodes stop Alex before she got away, he'd made himself stand still and endure the good-natured banter.

By the time he'd finally broken loose, he'd felt like an over-wound spring.

Peggy, the Slave Mistress, had come running up to him, as he started off the stage.

"You see?" she'd crowed happily. "What did I tell you, handsome? You didn't have a thing to worry about."

"What's her name?" he'd asked, and Peggy must have heard the tightness in his voice because she hadn't teased him or laughed, she'd simply said she'd asked the same question.

"Alexandra Thorpe."

"Married? Or single?"

"I don't know."

He'd nodded his thanks and begun to turn away when Peggy put her hand on his arm.

"Handsome?"

"Yes?" he'd said, impatiently.

"She's not for you."

"Yeah. Thanks for the advice."

"I'm serious. Remember what I said about her being an Ice Princess?"

Travis had looked squarely at Peggy. "You were wrong."

"No. No, I wasn't. Girl who told me the lady's name said she's got a freezer where her heart's supposed to be."

Travis had smiled. "It's not the lady's heart I'm interested in," he'd said, and then he'd gone down into the crowd, barely acknowledging the slaps on the back and the cheers from Pete Haskell and the other guys he worked with, pushing through everybody until, at last, he'd reached the lobby—and saw Alexandra Thorpe.

She'd still been talking with the chairwoman. Her back was to him, and he'd treated himself to the pleasure of the view. All that golden hair, streaming over her shoulders. The straight, elegant back, naked almost to the base of her spine. The gently rounded bottom, outlined in the silk garnet skirt. And those legs, those endless legs, encased in black hose that tapered down to shoes with heels high enough to make a man's mouth water.

He'd wondered what he'd find beneath that sinful excuse of a dress, when he took it off her later tonight. A black lace bra, with a matching garter belt? A scrap of silk that might be called a pair of panties?

Travis had felt his body tighten.

Or would there be nothing under that dress except the garter belt, and the sexy stockings?

His fingers itched with the need to find out.

He'd started toward her, then slowed his pace.

Something was wrong. It was in the set of her shoulders, the tilt of her head. He'd looked past the Thorpe woman, to the gray-haired chairwoman. She was smiling but there was no mistaking the earnest look on her face. She was making some sort of pitch.

He got closer, and heard enough to know he was right.

"It will only take a few minutes," she was saying. "If you and your bachelor could give the TV people a few pictures and a short interview, it would be wonderful publicity for the auction."

"He's not 'my' bachelor," Alexandra Thorpe had said. "You don't understand, Mrs. Rhodes. I'm not staying. Really, I can't."

Travis had stepped up behind her and told her that she could stay, that she *would* stay. For some reason, he'd gone heavy on the Texas drawl that was always just a heartbeat away. "Sugar," he'd called her, liking the way her eyes flared a little at the name. She'd been off balance, fighting something inside her—and then, suddenly, it had all changed.

It had been like seeing a woman pull a veil over her face. Or a mask. Yeah, that was it. Alexandra Thorpe had disappeared behind a mask, and it wasn't the first time it had happened tonight. It was just that he'd misread it, before. She hadn't gone from naked longing to confusion, she'd gone from longing to disbelief. Either she didn't know she was capable of that kind of desire or she didn't want to know it. Now, she was covering it with her Lady of the Manor act.

Covering, and she'd blamed him for it.

Instinct, as well as anger, urged him to take her in his arms and kiss that haughty smile from her face. With an arrogance that was more than a match for hers, he knew he could not only make her want him again, but he could make her beg him for the release only he could bring her, once she was in his arms.

Intelligence—what little he had left of it, considering the way his hormones were pumping—warned him that to do so would be a mistake. The thing to do was play along and see where Alexandra Thorpe imagined this would end.

Polite applause sprang up as she led him to the center of the dance floor. Barbara Rhodes must have seen them coming. The orchestra stopped in midbeat, and the chairwoman took hold of the microphone.

"Ladies and gentlemen, I am delighted to give you Ms. Alexandra Thorpe and her prize!"

Laugher, and more applause. Alex smiled and turned toward Travis, but her smile faltered when she saw the way he was looking at her. The orchestra began playing. The music was lush and romantic. Travis reached out and gathered her into his arms.

"Are you a good dancer, Ms. Thorpe?" he said softly. "Do you know how to let your body find the right rhythm?"

"I'm an excellent dancer. But I don't like to be held so tightly."

Travis smiled and drew her closer. "You seem stiff in my arms. Is it because you haven't—" his pause was slow and deliberate "—because you haven't—danced—enough, lately?"

Alex colored. "I don't know what you mean."

"Maybe you haven't had the right man. To dance with, I mean."

Her color deepened. What pleasure it was, to chip away at that arrogant composure and autocratic veneer.

"I could lead you in steps you've only dreamed of, Ms. Thorpe. All you have to do is admit that you want me for your teacher."

"That's enough!"

Alex tried to pull back but Travis's arm tightened around her. "Why did you pay twenty thousand bucks for me, Sugar?" He smiled through his teeth. "Your face is like an open book, Ms. Thorpe. You're torn between wanting to sock me in the jaw and turning tail and running like a scared rabbit."

"I never run from anything." Alex's voice hummed with fury. "But you've certainly got the first part right."

"Either way, five hundred people are watching us. And there's a TV camera pointed in our direction. Do you really want to make headlines, Ms. Thorpe?"

"You're a horrible man!"

"I'm an honest one. You paid a lot of money for me, and it didn't have a damned thing to do with charity."

"You overestimate your charm, sir."

"You paid it so you could go to bed with a man who'd make you feel something. And then you turned chicken."

Alex stopped moving. Travis did, too. She looked up at him, eyes blazing. "I really, really despise you!"

Travis laughed. "Ah, darlin', where's all that hauteur gone to? I know that's a mighty big word for a cowboy to use but I never said I was a cowboy, Ms. Thorpe. You were the one who decided that."

The music changed, became a waltz. Travis began moving in time with it. There was no choice. Alexandra began moving, too.

He circled the room with her in his arms, faster and faster, holding her so that her body was pressed to his. Her breasts, her thighs... God, how he wanted her. He could almost feel the heat of her, burning his skin. Yes, hatred blazed in her eyes but he knew women, and desire. And he could see something more in those eyes, besides hatred.

"What are you afraid to admit, Alex?"

His whisper was velvet-soft. Alex felt breathless. How had this happened? How had he taken control?

"I'm not afraid of anything." Even she could hear the tremor in her voice.

"Then tell me the truth," he said roughly. "Admit that you want me."

"I don't!"

Travis laughed. "Liar," he said, and whirled her faster and faster.

CHAPTER THREE

I T WAS a hell of a time to think of Jonas, but suddenly his father's voice was in his head.

"So now you think you're gonna fight for truth and justice," he'd said, the day Travis had been admitted to the Bar. "Well, lemme tell you somethin', boy. Only winners get justice, and liars never see the truth until you rub their noses in it."

For the first time, Travis decided Jonas might be right. There was only one thing to do, and he did it. He danced Alexandra Thorpe into a corner, bent her over his arm, and crushed her mouth beneath his.

He heard the insulted hiss of her breath, felt her first frantic struggles...and then, with a little sigh, she parted her lips and let him in.

He whispered her name, drew her up, gathered her into his arms. Her heart raced against his; her slender arms were cool as she looped them around his neck. She tasted like honey; she smelled like springtime. God, how he wanted her. How he needed her...

A cheer. A smattering of applause. Appreciative, pleasant laughter.

He heard them, but he didn't give a damn. Alex did. She tore her mouth from his, dropped her arms and flattened her palms against his chest.

"Stop it," she hissed.

He lifted his head and gave her a sexy smile that said the kiss was only the beginning. And why wouldn't he? Alex shuddered. She'd been kissing him the way she'd never kissed a man in her life, but he had no way of knowing that. Kissing him right here, in front of all these people.

He smiled into her eyes. "It's going to be one hell of a weekend, Sugar."

His voice was low, rough, and filled with promise. He was still holding her, his hands at her waist, which was a good thing because she felt boneless. Dizzy. She felt—she felt...

"Alex? Travis? Could you look this way, please?"

Alex swung around blindly. The TV camera was pointed at her; a smiling reporter poked a microphone into her face. She had always thought it was horrible, how intrusive reporters could be. Now, she welcomed the woman as if the microphone were a lifeline.

"Yes," she said brightly, and stepped free of Travis's grasp, "certainly. We'd be delighted."

The interview went on for what seemed to be hours, though Travis knew it could not have been more than a few minutes.

He didn't like reporters. There'd always been somebody poking a nose and a camera where it didn't belong when he was growing up on Espada. His father relished being the center of attention but neither Travis, his brothers nor his stepsister enjoyed it at all.

Tonight, Travis found himself welcoming—well, almost welcoming—the stupid questions and the phony smiles.

Alexandra Thorpe was doing most of the talking. She made it sound as if their kiss had been a clever piece of theatrics, hinting, with smiles and girlish laughter, that the two of them had planned it while they'd been talking in the lobby.

Whatever spin she wanted to put on it was fine with him. If she could come up with something clever, amen. Hey, he wasn't thinking at all. Near as he could tell, his brain had ceased to function as soon as he'd taken his first look at her.

He liked women, liked to come on to them. The delicacy of their bones. The subtlety of their scent. The way they laughed, and smiled. He enjoyed their company, their conversation. And making love with a woman was the closest to paradise a man could come.

The thing was, though, he never made love with an audience watching.

What was the sense in kidding himself? He wasn't just brain dead, he was being led around by the part of his anatomy that was the least reliable, to do what he'd been doing to Alexandra Thorpe, right in the middle of the dance floor. That kiss had been as erotic as anything he'd ever shared with a woman in the privacy of a bed.

Be honest, Baron. Some of the things he'd done in bed hadn't been as erotic as that kiss.

It had been that way for her, too. He knew what that sexy little moan had meant, knew from the feel of her in his arms that she'd been as ready as he'd been. He understood the touch of her tongue against his, the gentle pressure of her teeth...

"...Mr. Baron?"

He blinked. The ditzy reporter was talking to him, holding out her mike as if it were the Holy Grail.

"Excuse me?" he said, and she smiled even more brightly and repeated her question.

He smiled back. Yes, uh-huh, he'd had a great time tonight. No, of course he hadn't been nervous. Who could be nervous, when it was all for charity?

They were going to love this interview, at Sullivan, Cohen and Vittali.

Now it was Alexandra's turn. The reporter turned her painted-on smile in her direction.

"And what brought you here this evening, Ms. Thorpe?"

Alexandra hesitated for a second, then began talking about her lifelong commitment to charity. Travis pretended to listen, and smiled like an idiot. If she wasn't lying, he was a monkey's uncle.

Whatever had brought her here tonight didn't have anything to do with charity. He'd seen the look on her face, the wildness in her eyes. Something had driven her to this auction, and he needed to know what that something was.

But what had made her bid on him was easy to figure.

It had been desire. A desire that raged so fiercely within her that he'd felt its force on the stage. The same desire that had made her melt in his arms moments ago when he'd kissed her.

That first rigidity of her body, and then the way she'd shuddered and come alive in his arms. The feel of her breasts, pressed against his chest. Her lips, parting to give him access to the honeyed essence of her mouth. The whisper of sound that had spoken of surrender...

He knew he'd never forget it. There was no point pretending he didn't have a long history with women. Still, that kiss, that incredible kiss, was different from anything he'd ever known.

Travis shifted his weight. What was he doing to himself? Another couple of seconds, the TV camera and the crowd were going to be treated to a sight he'd never live down. It was time to take this strange little play to a private setting, where the next scene could be played out, in full.

He slipped his arm around Alexandra's waist, his hand splaying against her hip in warning.

"Okay," he said cheerfully, breaking into the middle of some inanity of the reporter. "Okay, folks, that's it."

The little knot of journalists groaned. One of them began to ask another question but Travis just kept smiling. And talking.

"Hey, guys, don't you think Ms. Thorpe and I are entitled to a little time alone?"

"You have a three-day weekend to be alone," one of them said, and they all laughed.

"And a weekend to plan," Travis said. He looked down at Alex. "Right, Ms. Thorpe?"

"Right, Mr. Baron," she said, flashing him a smile that was vaguely reminiscent of the snarl of an angry Doberman.

"I just love that old-fashioned formality," the reporter gushed. "Mr., Ms.... So charming!"

Travis laughed merrily as he began backing Alex from the dance floor. "Well," he said, "Ms. Thorpe is just an old-fashioned girl."

As if on cue, the orchestra struck up another waltz. Come on, Travis thought, come on!

People surged onto the floor to dance.

Travis didn't waste any time. He let go of Alexandra's waist, grabbed her hand and all but sprinted for the door. She tried to tug free when they were halfway through the lobby but his fingers tightened on hers.

"Keep going," he said, and led her out the main doors, past the doorman and down the wide marble steps. Anybody watching would figure they were making a romantic getaway. He almost imagined it, himself, until they reached the street and she dug in her spiked heels, wrenched her hand from his and spun toward him.

"Exactly what do you think you're doing?" she said, turning her angry face up to his.

"Calm down, Sugar."

Alexandra stamped her foot. "Kindly do not 'sugar' me!"

"My car is parked just up the street."

"Do you really think I give a damn where your car is parked?" Alex tossed her head. "Listen to me, Mr. Baron, and listen well. You are, without question, the most horrible man I ever—"

Travis rolled his eyes, grabbed her wrist and tugged her down the street and into a doorway.

"Don't you ever think before you make a scene, lady? Or do you like being in the spotlight?"

"I cherish my privacy."

"Yeah, well, you've got a strange way of showing it." He waved his hand in the general direction of the main entrance to the Hotel Paradise. "What makes you so sure that nitwit reporter and her bozo cameraman weren't hot on our heels, huh?''

He could see her face pale a little, even in the darkness of the doorway.

''Were they?''

He leaned out and looked. ''No,'' he snapped. ''But you didn't even think about it before you started chewing me out. Just once, you might try thinking of the consequences before you act.''

''Me? Me, think of the consequences?'' Alex threw back her head. ''Ha,'' she said, without the least touch of humor, ''oh, ha, Mr. Baron, that is a good one! That's really something, coming from you.''

Travis folded his arms. ''I,'' he said loftily, ''am not the person who got us into this mess.''

And now that he thought about it, it *was* a mess. He'd made an idiot of himself, prancing around onstage. And then the Thorpe babe had made an idiot of herself, running away. And just now—he'd kissed her in front of a zillion people in a way he'd probably never, ever live down.

''I am the innocent party in this entire unfortunate affair, sir!''

''Hey, Sugar. Don't you pull that Ice Princess bit on me.''

''Are you deaf, Mr. Baron? Do not call me 'sugar.' ''

''Forgive me, *Ms.* Thorpe!'' His mouth thinned and he shoved his face toward hers. Despite herself, Alex took a hurried step back. ''Princess suits you,'' he muttered. ''That little lady'll never know how right she was!''

''What little lady?''

''Never mind.'' A muscle knotted in Travis's cheek. ''The bottom line here is that I am tired of being the villain in this piece.''

''Are you suggesting that I am?''

''*You* bid on me, remember?''

Color shot into her face. ''Permit me to refresh your memory, Mr. Baron. This was a bachelor auction. The whole purpose of the event was for women to bid on men.''

"Uh-huh."

"What, pray tell, is that supposed to mean?"

"It means you didn't have to bid so much for me that you brought the house down."

"I don't have to listen to this—"

Travis grabbed her shoulder as Alex tried to brush past him. "And then," he growled, "as if you hadn't drawn enough attention to us already—"

"*I* drew attention?" Alex tossed back her head and laughed. "Oh, I love that, Mr. Baron. *I* wasn't up on that stage, prancing around like a—a male stripper!"

A smile tilted across Travis's mouth. He shifted his weight so that he blocked the doorway. All Alex could see were his broad shoulders and his ruggedly handsome face, only that and the dark night that surrounded them.

Her heart skipped a beat.

They were on a street in a busy city but she suddenly felt as if they were the last man and woman on Earth. It was the same way she'd felt when, with bravado in her blood and idiocy in her brain, she'd burst into the ballroom and spotted him onstage. The same way she'd felt on the dance floor, when he'd kissed her.

"Exactly how many male strippers have you watched in your time, Ms. Thorpe?" he said softly.

"Mr. Baron." Her voice squeaked. She cleared her throat and began again. "Mr. Baron, really. I think we should just call it a night and—" Alex caught her breath. Travis had caught a strand of her hair between his fingers. She watched, wide-eyed, as he drew it to his nostrils. "What—what are you doing?"

"I like the smell of your hair, Princess. What is that? Opium? Joy?"

"It's—it's just…" She stepped back again as he moved closer. Her shoulders hit the closed door behind her. "I—I don't remember." She didn't, either. She couldn't think straight. Was that breathless little voice really hers? And was she really trembling? Alex shut her eyes, moaned as Travis touched his lips to her throat. "Mr. Baron..."

"Under the circumstances," Travis said huskily, "I really think we might move on to first names. Don't you, Ms. Thorpe?"

Didn't she what? Alex shuddered as his breath warmed her skin. She couldn't think, not while he was—while he was...

"Mr. Baron—"

"Travis."

"Travis. Travis, really, I think—"

"Yeah. So do I." His arms went around her. He gathered her against him, her breasts against the hard wall of his chest, her thighs against his. She put her hands out to ward him off. Instead, somehow, they curled into the lapels of his tuxedo. "I think it's time I kissed you again, Princess, but without an audience."

His mouth came down on hers.

"No," she whispered, "please..."

"Let go, Princess." He kissed her, soft, gentle kisses that made her lips cling to his. "Just let go and do what you want to do."

His hand slid up, captured her breast, his thumb moving across the silk-covered nipple. And, for the second time that night—for the second time in her entire life—Alex did what she had never done before.

She let go.

She gave a little cry so wild and plaintive it made his blood quicken. And wrapped her arms around his neck as she rose on her toes and tilted her pelvis against his.

Travis groaned. His mouth slanted hungrily over hers, his tongue seeking and finding access to the silken sweetness of hers. He slipped his hands down her body, following the narrowness of her waist, the soft curve of her hips, and cupped her bottom, lifting her into the hardness of his arousal, moving against her as she cried out against his mouth.

"Alex," he whispered.

"Yes," she sighed, "oh, yes."

He kissed her shoulder, bit the flesh, bent his head further and sucked the silk-covered center of her breast into his mouth. His hands swept up her thighs, under her skirt; she was wearing what he'd dreamed she was wearing, just those sexy stockings, a scrap of lace and nothing more. He said something she couldn't understand, thrust his hand beneath the lace and cupped her.

She was hot. Wet. The aroused smell of her fueled him with desire. Her sobbing little breaths torched him with flame. And when she kissed his throat, sank her teeth into his flesh, he knew his need for this woman was greater than his need for breath.

He clasped her hand and brought it to him. She groaned and curved her fingers around him and he felt the blood begin to pool in his loins.

"Alex," he said harshly.

"Please," she whispered, "oh, please, please, please..."

He knew he could have her, now. Right here, right in this doorway. All he had to do was unzip his fly, rip away that bit of lace, bury himself deep inside her...

Someone laughed. Alex heard it, and froze. Travis did, too.

"Oh God," she whispered.

He put his arms around her. She was trembling. "Easy," he said softly.

The laughter came again, good-natured and distant. He realized it had nothing to do with them. It was coming from somewhere up the street, though it had gotten closer. And then the haze that clouded his brain cleared and he realized that he was standing in a doorway with a woman he'd met less than two hours ago, and there were cars passing by and pedestrians on the sidewalk and he was—he'd been about to—

She must have realized it, too. "Let me go," she whispered frantically, and began struggling to free herself of his embrace.

Travis held her tighter.

"Damn you, let me—"

"Hold still!"

It was a command, not a request. And a logical one. People were coming; Alex could hear them. With luck, if neither she nor Travis moved, whomever was approaching would pass by without noticing them. So she stiffened in his arms and tried not to think about what this—this stranger had been doing to her, seconds ago, what she'd been letting him do.

And for what? To prove that Carl was wrong? That she wasn't—wasn't a frigid little rich bitch?

Alex's stomach took a tumble. She closed her eyes. All right. She'd proved it, in the most humiliating way possible. Proved it to herself and to this man she didn't know, a man who surely hadn't turned her on, who'd simply been in the right place at the right time when she was in desperate need of pretending she could feel desire...

The footsteps and voices were just beyond the doorway. Alex trembled.

"It's all right," Travis whispered, and drew her against him.

And she let him do it. Let him stroke his hand up and down her spine, until she felt boneless. Let him thread his fingers into her hair and gently bury her face against his throat. Against the hot, masculine skin she'd tasted and wanted to taste again. Against that swift-beating pulse that mirrored hers. Against that hard, powerful body she yearned to explore, against that terrifying, exhilarating, exciting arousal...

A sound broke from Alex's throat and she tore herself from Travis's arms.

"I'm sure the women you usually keep company with enjoy this sort of thing, Mr. Baron."

Travis blinked. "What?"

"The—the primitive approach. It must wow them, back in—in Little Rock. Or—or Dallas. Or wherever it is you come from."

His eyes narrowed as they focused on her icy features. "Hey, babe, take it easy. I don't know what your problem is, but don't take it out on me."

"Probably sweeps them off their feet, in cow country. But this is Los Angeles, sir. And I'd appreciate it if you'd just get out of my way."

Travis's mouth thinned. "Get out of your way?" he said, slowly and softly.

"How nice to know you don't have a hearing problem, Mr. Baron. Yes. Get out of my way. Now."

His vision grew dark. He felt the surge of his blood as the most primal of instincts took over, urging him to do what he longed to do to Alex Thorpe, what any man would want to do, and teach her a lesson she'd never forget.

"There's a name for women like you," he said. "And I'm sure you've heard it many times before."

He watched her face go white, braced himself for the sting of her hand against his jaw…but it didn't happen. She simply stood very still, her body as rigid as a marble column. Then, to his amazement, she smiled.

"Believe me," she said softly, "I've been called worse."

Her voice quavered on the last word but she kept smiling. It was that brave, sad smile that defeated him, made him wish to God he could call back the ugly words he'd used but it was too late. Alex Thorpe stepped past him, onto the sidewalk just as a cruising taxi came by.

"Alex," Travis called, "Princess, wait…"

She stepped into the cab, the door shut and the taxi roared off into the night.

CHAPTER FOUR

TRAVIS paced the floor of his home on the beach at Malibu.

He was angry, restless—and frustrated.

What had made him think he owed Alexandra Thorpe an apology? Okay, he'd called her something pretty lousy but, dammit, it was a name she more than deserved. And what had made him behave like such a jerk? He'd acted like a monkey on a stick all night, jumping in whatever direction she'd wanted. Turn him on, turn him off...

"What does she think I am?" he muttered. "A light switch?"

He paced some more, opened the glass sliders that led from his bedroom to the deck and glowered at the Pacific Ocean.

The whole thing was ridiculous. The auction. The bidding. Her behavior, his behavior...

He swore and stomped back into the bedroom. He tugged off his boots, yanked off his tie, dumped his tux and everything that went with it on the floor and kicked the entire mess into the corner, in the process stubbing his toe on the corner of the bed.

"Bull-spit," he roared, and danced around the room on one foot. He limped to the dresser, took out a pair of running shorts and a Texas Longhorns T-shirt and pulled them on. His toe still hurt but he didn't much care. Pain was a part of running, anyway, he told himself grimly, and set out for a hard five miles on the packed sand.

He was panting when he got back, and sweat-drenched. But he felt better. Most definitely better.

"Goodbye, Ice Princess," he said as he dumped his

shorts and T-shirt on the tiled floor and stepped into the shower.

He loved this shower. Sybaritic, Slade had said, the first time he saw it, and yeah, it probably was. An overhead spray. Two side sprays. A marble bench. And room enough for two...

For two. For Alex, and for him. Travis closed his eyes and imagined what it would be like to soap that beautiful body. To cup her naked breasts. To bend his head and taste them, to hear her breathy little sighs as she wrapped her arms around his neck and her legs around his hips, to pin her back against the glass wall while the water beat down like warm rain as he buried himself deep inside her slick heat...

He groaned, looked down at himself in dismay and turned the shower to icy-cold.

Dressed again, this time in jeans and a white T-shirt, his feet bare, Travis went into the kitchen and took a can of Coke from the refrigerator. It was late. Or early, depending on your point of view. The glass walls of his house looked out on a beach silent and deserted in the early morning.

Damn, he still felt restless. He needed a cigarette, but he'd given them up five years ago. He needed a cold beer or a glass of decent wine, but there was no beer in the fridge and he wasn't in the mood to check the wine rack. He needed to talk to one of his brothers, but what would he say to them? That he was furious and frustrated, and pacing the floor like a teenage kid?

What he needed was a woman. One who wouldn't turn him on and off like a faucet, who wouldn't drive him crazy. Who'd be honest about wanting to share his bed. That would put Alex Thorpe out of his head, once and for all.

Travis reached for his address book and thumbed through the pages. He'd met a gorgeous brunette just last week and said he'd call her. She'd probably be surprised to hear from him at this hour but he'd invite her to breakfast on the beach. Champagne. Caviar and scrambled eggs...

Who was he kidding? Dammit, he thought, and tossed the book aside. He didn't want a substitute for the Ice Princess. He wanted her.

Where was she now? He didn't even have her address or her phone number. What was she doing? Was she sleeping, dreaming of him? Or was she going crazy, the way he was, remembering...

The doorbell rang. Travis had never been so glad to have his train of thought interrupted. He went to the door, opened it and found a kid in an olive-drab uniform on the porch.

"Morning, sir. I have a delivery for Mr. Travis Baron."

"Great," Travis said briskly, signed his name to a receipt and took five bucks out of his pocket. "Thanks."

He shut the door, shot a puzzled glance at the package the kid had handed him and tore it open. A small vellum envelope, with his name elegantly scripted across the front, fell out.

Travis picked it up, frowned, examined it. He raised it to his nose and sniffed, but no perfume scent clung to the paper. What was inside? Something formal. An invitation? A thank-you? It might be either one, if Alex Thorpe...

Man, he was really losing it! No way the Thorpe babe would write him a note. The only envelope she'd send him would probably blow him to smithereens the second he opened it.

Smiling, he opened the vellum envelope and took out a note-card.

"Oh, hell," Travis said, and groaned.

Your presence is requested at
The eighty-fifth birthday celebration
Of Mr. Jonas Baron
Saturday and Sunday, June 14 and 15
At the Baron Ranch
"Espada"
Brazos Springs, Texas
RSVP

The script was handwritten and elegant but the message was a bummer. The sender knew it, too. The note, scrawled beneath the RSVP, made that clear.

"Yes, Travis," it read, "this means you!"

The words were followed by a bold capital *C,* and the drawing of a tiny heart.

He laughed. Caitlin. His little stepsister was some piece of work. Hard when she had to be, soft when she wanted to be. And, just now, she was going to be tough. This was no invitation, it was notice of a command performance. Just what he wanted, he thought wryly.

The old man, eighty-five? Wow. It was hard to believe. The last time he'd seen his father a year, two years ago, when Catie had conned them all into coming to the ranch for Thanksgiving or Christmas, some sort of holiday, Jonas had looked as tough and spare as ever. He certainly hadn't looked old. But he was; eighty-five years on this earth said it all.

But the party would just have to go on without him. No way was he flying to Texas in the middle of June for the privilege of subjecting himself to a weekend's worth of Jonas's sharp tongue...

A weekend with Catie, and Slade and Gage. A couple of days of reminiscing about the past, of maybe taking a swim down in the creek. Los Lobos style. Travis grinned. Well, Los Lobos style, pre-Catie. In those days, the Baron brothers used to swim bare-assed, proving their manhood by surviving the zillions of bloodthirsty, buzzard-size mosquitoes that swarmed from the banks along the stream.

A weekend like that might just clear his head.

Travis reached for the phone before he could change his mind, hit a speed dial button. Slade answered on the first ring.

"Slade, my man. How you doin'?"

In Boston, Slade Baron plucked a duplicate vellum invitation from the top of his desk and grinned.

"I was doin' fine, until a messenger turned up at my door this mornin'."

Travis chuckled. "Our Catie, efficient as always. She even took the time difference into consideration. I'll bet Gage is lookin' at this bombshell right about now, same as us."

"Yeah. Well, I'd have called you, anyway. That auction was last night, wasn't it?"

Travis frowned. "So?"

"Whoa, Trav, my man, don't be so testy. "

"I'm not being anything. I just want to discuss this invitation."

"Discuss it all you like, Trav. I ain't goin'."

"I'll just bet your high-priced architectural clients love that down-home talk," Travis said, and grinned.

"They're never lucky enough to hear it, and stop changing the subject. How'd the auction go?"

"It went. Somebody bought me."

"Lucky lady. She have a name?"

"Alexandra. And that's the end of the story."

"How much did you go for? More than the dude from that other law firm? Was this Alexandra good-lookin'?"

"I went for enough, I beat the pants off the other guy, the lady was okay, if you like the type."

"Oh, my."

"What's that supposed to mean?"

"Well, sounds to me as if my big brother struck out for a change."

"Think again, pal," Travis said, tossing off the lie with ease. It was better than having Slade pursue the subject, as he damned well knew he would. His kid brother could be worse than a hound on a trail, when he got started on something.

"Ah. So, she's there with you, huh?"

"You could say that, yeah."

Hell, it wasn't a lie. The Princess was inside his head,

wasn't she? As real as a woman could be, without being in a man's arms?

"Trav, you old dog, you."

Travis sighed. "Slade, do you think you could get your mind on something else?"

"You really want to talk about this birthday party, huh? Well, there's nothing to talk about. I'm not going. I already told you that."

"Jonas is coming up on eighty-five. It's a milestone."

"I don't care if it's a century stone. Why would any of us subject himself to a weekend of misery?"

"It won't be so awful."

"Says you."

"There'll probably be a couple of hundred people there. The old boy won't have the time to chew us up. Besides, I hate to disappoint Caitlin."

"What's with you, Trav? It almost sounds as if you're lookin' to get out of town."

Travis shut his eyes. If life had taught him anything, it was that there wasn't much one brother could hide from another.

"Well, I wouldn't mind a change of scene."

"Woman trouble," Slade said, and sighed.

"Yeah. I guess."

"I might have known."

"You? No way," Travis said, with forced lightness. "Gage and I are the ones who know about women, except Gage doesn't really count, considering that he's the only one who's still married."

"You're trying to change the subject, Trav."

Travis gave a little laugh. "Right. I am. And before you ask, trust me, kid. You don't want to hear the gory details. Look, about this party—"

"Listen, I'm sorry, but I'm not going. I really don't have time to go back to Espada right now, okay?"

"That's that, then. Heck, you're too big for me to lock in the feed bin anymore." The brothers chuckled, and then

Travis cleared his throat. "Do me a favor, will you? Stay on the line while I phone Gage."

"Two against one won't do it anymore," Slade said, and laughed. "Even if Gage says he's going, with bells on, I'm not changing my mind."

"Fair enough, but say 'hello' to him anyway," Travis said, and punched in his other brother's private number.

Gage picked up on the first ring. "Baby," he said gruffly, "Natalie, I love you so—"

Travis laughed. "I love you, too, precious," he said in a high falsetto, "but my husband's starting to get suspicious."

"Travis? Is that you?"

"And me," Slade said lazily. "How are you, bro?"

"I don't believe this! What are you guys doin'? Havin' a reunion out there in California? Or are you both in Boston, livin' it up in that mansion my little brother calls home?"

Travis chuckled. "This three-way brotherly phone call is comin' to you courtesy of the marvels of modern-day science."

"And it's probably the only three-way ever done by telephone," Slade said, with a wicked grin at the pretty young secretary who'd just brought him his coffee. "Thank you, darlin'."

"Don't you darlin' me, pal," Travis said, with a mock growl, "or I'll fly straight to that fancy-pants mansion of yours and beat you up the way I used to, when you were twelve and I was thirteen."

"Uh-huh. You an' who else?"

"Me an' Gage." Travis grinned. "'Course, it'll have to wait until the sun gets up in the sky a piece, so my brain starts workin' right."

All three brothers laughed. Travis punched the pillows behind him and sat back. He felt better already. There was nothing like shared memories, even the bad ones, and the thought was enough to make him remember the reasons for this phone call.

"Okay, guys," he said. "I wish to hell we could avoid the topic but it's time for a reality check."

"The invitation," Slade said.

Gage sighed. "You got yours, too?"

"This morning, bright and early, same as Trav."

"Bright and early is right. Mine arrived at six," Travis said.

"Yeah." Slade laughed. "And interrupted you and your guest. Isn't that right, Trav?"

Travis shut his eyes and rubbed his forehead with his fist. "Oh, yeah," he said briskly, and choked out a laugh. "There's nothing like being awakened with an invitation to purgatory when you, uh, when you, when you're otherwise involved."

Gage and Slade laughed. "What a tough life he leads," Slade drawled.

"I'd expect some compassion from you, kid," Travis said, and quickly took the conversation elsewhere. "None from Gage, of course. He gave up his freedom years ago." His voice softened. "How's my girl, by the way? You still treating her right, or is she about ready to use that pretty head of hers and ditch you for me?"

"She's fine."

Travis's brows lifted. His brother's tone seemed strained. "You sure?"

"Yeah," Slade said. "You don't sound…"

"Listen, maybe you guys can horse around all day," Gage snapped, "but I've got things to do."

"Right," Slade said, after a minute. "Uh, look, Trav's already laid out the agenda. What are we going to do about this command performance the old man's got planned for the middle of the month?"

"Ignore it," Gage said firmly. "I've got—"

"Things to do," Travis said. "Yeah, I know. And I don't have any greater desire to go back to Espada for a dress rehearsal of King Lear than either of you guys, but—"

"Lear?" Slade said, sounding puzzled. "Hey, this is Texas we're talking about, not Stratford-on-Avon."

"Come on, Slade, you know what this is all about." Travis frowned and wondered how come he hadn't seen it sooner. "Jonas is starting to feel mortal."

"Our father's figuring on making it to one hundred, and you know what? My money's on him."

"Yeah, but I bet the old boy's looking around, taking stock of that little spread of seven zillion acres he calls home, sweet home, and figuring it's time he made plans on how to divvy up the kingdom."

"Well, I don't need to spend a miserable weekend on Espada to know that I don't give a damn how he does it," Gage said gruffly. "You two enjoy the party without me."

"Hold it right there, pal." Slade's voice rang with indignation. "I'm going to be in Baltimore that weekend."

"Or in the Antarctic," Travis said lazily, "anywhere it takes to avoid this shindig, right?"

"Wrong. I put in eight weeks on plans for a new bank, and I am not going to—"

"Dammit, Slade..." Travis took a deep breath, then blew it out. "Sorry, kid. I have no right to twist your arm."

"Forget it. Truth is, I was lying through my teeth. I could get out of the Baltimore thing, if I wanted."

"Amazing," Gage said softly. "Three grown men, all of us falling over our own feet in a rush to keep clear of the place where we grew up."

They talked some more, even laughed a little. Then Travis cleared his throat.

"The thing is, eighty-five is a pretty impressive number."

"The old man was never impressed by other numbers," Gage said bitterly. "Your eighteenth birthday. Slade's two years in grad school."

"Or your big fifth anniversary party," Travis said, "but what the hell, gentlemen, we're bigger than that, right?" Groans greeted the announcement, but Travis was undeterred. "We're young, he's old. That's a simple fact." His voice softened. "And then there's Caitlin."

"Yeah." Slade sighed. "I do hate to disappoint her."

"Me, too. But I just don't see a choice here," Gage muttered.

"Exactly," Travis said, in the tone of reason that had made him such a successful attorney. "There isn't any choice. The way I see it, we have to show up."

"No way," two voices said, in unison.

"Look, we're not kids anymore. Jonas can't get under our skin and make us miserable." Travis paused. He was pushing, he knew, but Catie really would be heartbroken if they didn't show. And, dammit, selfish or not, he needed this weekend with his brothers. "Think of the plus side. We get to swap war stories and put a smile on Catie's face at the same time. Is that really so much to ask?"

There was a long silence, and then Slade sighed. "Okay, count me in."

"Not me," Gage said. "I don't have a weekend to spare."

"Gage," Travis said, "look—"

"No, you look! I'm too busy for this stuff. I have some sensitive things going on here. You got that, or do I have to put it on a billboard in Times... Oh, hell. I'm sorry. I didn't mean to yell. But I can't go. I just can't."

"Sure," Travis said, after a minute.

"Understood," Slade said, a beat later. "Well..."

There was silence, the sound of a throat being cleared. "Well," three voices said, and then there were hurried goodbyes and the brothers all disconnected. Travis waited a couple of seconds, then punched in Gage's number.

"Listen," he said, as soon as he heard his brother's voice, "if there's a problem on your end—"

Gage, sounding matter-of-fact, assured him there wasn't.

"Yeah, well, if there should be—"

"I'll call you."

Travis nodded, hit his phone's Off button, then waited for it to ring.

"I called him back," Slade said, without bothering to say hello.

"Uh-huh. So did I."

"Something's wrong, Trav. I've never heard Gage sound like that."

"Yeah. But whatever it is, he doesn't want to talk about it."

"Trav? You don't think there could be trouble between Gage and Natalie, do you?"

"No way. That marriage was made in heaven. Natalie's wonderful." Travis's tone flattened. "She's not the sort of woman who'd ever make a man jump through hoops. She's like an open book. No games, no secrets…"

"Tell me about it," Slade said, with a little laugh.

"They're all impossible." Travis leaned his elbows on the deck's cedar railing. "They run hot, they run cold. A man never knows what to expect."

"You've got that right," Slade said darkly. "No matter what you say or do, it's never enough." He hesitated. "So, are we talking about your ex?"

"No, we're not. And, before you ask, I don't feel like discussing it any further."

"Suit yourself, pal."

"Slade?" Travis's voice softened. "I'm looking forward to seeing you, kid."

He could almost see his brother smile. "Yeah," Slade said gruffly, "me, too."

Travis hung up and walked out on the deck. It was a beautiful morning. Bright sunshine, blue sky, and the aqua waters of the ocean rolling out toward infinity. He felt better, now that he'd spoken with his brothers. And he was glad he hadn't asked a woman to join him here. Whatever else he was when it came to women, he wasn't a user. He never took more than he gave.

It was too bad the same couldn't be said of Alexandra Thorpe.

Travis's expression hardened. Was that what the Thorpe babe did for kicks? Offered a man a glimpse of Paradise, teased him until he went beyond caring, beyond sanity, then turned and walked away?

It was a dangerous thing to do, something that could turn violent if she picked the wrong guy. But she probably chose her victims carefully. They wouldn't be bar pickups, or men she met in casual encounters. There were too many unknowns that way. She would come on to men like him, ones who were successful and prominent. Men she could toy with but not fear.

His mouth narrowed. He'd never understood it, when men said they knew just what a woman needed, but he understood it now. He could feel the tension twisting inside him again. Calm down, he told himself. Take it easy...

The hell with that. The Ice Princess had picked the wrong sucker this time. Travis went back into the bedroom and reached for the phone.

She wasn't listed, but he hadn't expected her to be. Barbara Rhodes was. If she was surprised to hear from him so early in the morning, she covered it well, but she couldn't disguise her surprise at his request.

"I'm not supposed to do this, Mr. Baron," she said.

"Of course not," Travis said pleasantly. "And it shouldn't be necessary. Ms. Thorpe gave me her address and phone number on a scrap of paper but I managed to misplace it." He dropped his voice and did his best to sound boyish, and charming. "I'm sure you understand that I wouldn't want her to know that."

Minutes later, Travis was in his Porsche, roaring along the back roads toward the canyons high above Los Angeles.

CHAPTER FIVE

HIGH above Eagle Canyon, in a house her grandfather had built and her father, and then her husband, had dominated, Alexandra Thorpe was having breakfast in her garden.

Having breakfast in her garden was a first-time event, one Alex was savoring with almost guilty pleasure.

She had slept badly. She'd tossed and turned and dreamed, though she couldn't remember what she'd dreamed, only that she'd come awake, heart-racing, somewhere around five-thirty.

Enough, she'd thought firmly, was enough and, since it was so early, she'd come down the ornate staircase of Thorpe House still in her nightgown, then padded barefoot across the cold stone floor of the huge entry hall, to the kitchen.

The big room was silent. Not even Luisa was stirring so early. Alex had taken a container of orange juice out of the refrigerator but when her gaze fell on a can of coffee, she knew that was what she really wanted. Still, she'd hesitated. The kitchen was the servants' domain. Well, Luisa's, now that her father was gone and Carl was, too, and she'd gotten rid of the maid and butler and chauffeur who'd made Thorpe House run. That the kitchen was off limits to Thorpes—and to Stuarts—wasn't a rule, it was simply an understanding.

Alex stood there, looking at the coffee can. Suddenly she reached for it.

"It's only coffee, Alex," she muttered impatiently.

She read the instructions with great concentration, then spent a few minutes searching for the filters. Minutes later, the coffee was gurgling merrily into its glass carafe in the pot on the granite counter.

"Understanding" number one broken, she'd thought, al-

55

most giddily. Why not number two? There really wasn't any reason to go back upstairs and dress. Luisa was still in her rooms. She was alone here. And surely somewhere on the West Coast of the United States, another woman was about to violate the laws of civilized behavior and have her breakfast in her nightgown.

Laughter bubbled up in her throat at the silly thought. Still smiling, she padded into the dining room, to set a place for herself at the enormous black walnut table. Just then, a finger of buttery-yellow sunlight had streamed through one of the arched windows.

"To hell with it," Alex had said to the dining room, and she'd marched back into the kitchen, made herself toast, poured juice, put a cup and the pot of freshly brewed coffee on a tray and carried it out to the tiled patio, to one of the glass tables that had never held anything but cocktails and hors d'oeuvres. Her father had thought eating out of doors was a lower-class convention. Her husband had thought it uncomfortable, and she didn't even want to think what either would have said about her sitting here, in her nightgown at six something in the morning, eating a breakfast she'd prepared with her own hands.

Orange juice had never tasted sweeter, or toast more crunchy. And the coffee, when she took a first, tentative sip, was rich and delicious on her tongue.

She held the cup in two hands, letting its warmth seep into her blood, and smiled. It was foolish to feel so good about such a little series of events, but she felt good about them, anyway, as if she were taking the first steps toward reclaiming her own life.

Alex's smile slipped.

She had to stop thinking about last night, that was all. What she'd done, what she might have done, with a stranger, in a doorway—a *doorway*—if she hadn't come to her senses, didn't matter. She had come to her senses; that was what mattered. Wasn't it?

"Good morning, *señora*."

Coffee sloshed over the rim of Alex's cup. "Luisa," she said, and forced a smile. "I hope you don't mind, but I invaded your kitchen."

Luisa minded. Alex could see it in the look that flashed over her face just before she covered it with a polite smile.

"Certainly not, Señora Stuart. But if the *señora* was hungry, she should have awakened me."

"There was no need. And, Luisa? I know I've mentioned this before... Would you please stop addressing me that way?"

"*Señora?*"

"I am Ms. Thorpe, Luisa. Or Ms. Alex. Or just Alex, if you like. But I am not 'Señora Stuart.'"

"Oh, of course." Luisa flushed. "It's just that it was your father's preference. And your—and Mr. Carl's."

"Yes, well it's not mine," Alex said, struggling to sound pleasant.

"I'll make it a point to remember. May I bring you anything else?"

"Nothing, thank you. I'll call if I need you, Luisa."

So much for "understanding" number four, Alex thought, as the patio door swung shut. Never surprise the servants. Well, she hadn't surprised Luisa, she'd shocked her. The truth was, she'd shocked herself, too. What was wrong with her this morning? She was feeling contrary. Restless. As if what she needed to do was turn the world upside down.

Alex lifted her cup to her lips.

She'd come close enough to doing just that, last night.

But that craziness, whatever it had been, was over. And she wasn't going to waste time thinking about it. It was just that she'd behaved so foolishly, setting herself up for one embarrassment after another from the moment she'd overheard those two harpies talking in the ladies' lounge at *L'Orangerie.*

Whatever had possessed her, to hurry to Saks and buy the clothing she'd already dumped in the corner of her closet? The lace that masqueraded as underwear. The garnet dress.

And... Alex blushed. And those—those come-and-get-me shoes? She groaned and put her hand to her forehead. All of that, and for what? To prove that she could turn a man on?

Color flooded her face.

How could she have planned something so sleazy? Bought a man. Let him—let him do things...

Oh, hell.

She shot to her feet and walked into the garden. It was her province. Neither her father nor Carl had understood why she'd want to get her hands dirty, tending her flowers, but they'd both tolerated it, even shared amused, masculine smiles over what they'd referred to as her hobby. But it was more than that, to Alex. There was something wonderfully restorative about trimming the impatiens or coaxing the roses to bloom. She loved the riot of colors, the crimsons and pinks and deep yellows. And the flowers' perfumes were wonderful, better by far than any of the scents trapped in the expensive designer vials lined up on the vanity table in her bedroom.

The impatiens were a bit ragged. Alex bent down and began snapping their heads. The phlox needed tending, too....

She went still. Then she puffed out her breath and stood up.

Who was she kidding? She could prepare a dozen more breakfasts, tend her flowers until the sun was high in the sky, but she still wouldn't get rid of the memories. Travis Baron was still lodged in her head, damn him. Those knowing eyes. That little smile. Was the humiliation of last night going to haunt her for the rest of her life?

Probably.

People had seen. Not what had happened in that doorway, thank goodness, but the rest of it—her outrageous bid, the way he'd held her when they danced, that kiss...

Oh, goodness, that kiss.

People had seen, and they'd talk. They'd laugh. They'd tease. And she'd have to laugh right along with them, smile and think of something suitably clever and outrageous to say so no one would have reason to imagine either the man or the kiss had meant anything to her, because they hadn't.

"They didn't," Alex said. She sat down at the table and picked up her cup.

Those things he'd done to her. Cheap things. Awful things. She'd never have let him do them, if she'd been thinking straight. What women would? Well, some women, maybe. But she was not one of them. And if Carl—if any man— wanted to call a woman frigid because she wouldn't lie and pretend sex was more than something—something men wanted that was vaguely unhygienic...well, that was the man's problem. Not the woman's.

No intelligent person could really believe that a woman who'd never cried out in a man's arms was, somehow, less than she might be.

She had cried out, though. Last night, in Travis Baron's arms, she'd cried out, she'd felt things, wanted things....

The cup shook in Alex's hand. She put it down carefully. There was no sense in thinking about it. Hadn't she wasted most of the night, doing exactly that? All the recriminations in the world wouldn't change what had happened.

"Well," she'd say, with a big smile, when people teased her, "it was for charity, after all."

There'd surely be those who'd noticed the way she was dressed, that she'd never worn anything so—so obvious in her life, but no one in her circle would be indiscreet enough to comment.

Not to her face, anyway.

And she'd survive. Thorpeses always did. People *would* forget, and so would she. Soon, she wouldn't remember any of the details of the night. None of them. Not Travis Baron's name, or his face, or the way he'd kissed her. Or the way that cruel-looking mouth had managed to take hers with such heart-stopping hunger. He'd be out of her head, out of her dreams...

Her dreams.

Alex folded her trembling hands in her lap. She had just remembered her dream. And, God, she wished she hadn't.

She'd dreamed she was standing in the entry hall of Thorpe House...

Only it wasn't Thorpe House. It was a castle, and she was alone in the hall, waiting for something. For someone. Her hair streamed over her shoulders. Her feet were bare. And her heart, beneath her plain white gown, beat so fast, so hard, she could feel it in her throat.

Suddenly, the massive doors of the castle burst open. A huge black charger filled the doorway. On its back was a knight in black armor. His hair was sun-gilded, his eyes emerald-green.

The Black Knight was Travis Baron, and he had come for her. He was heaven and earth, he was all the fires of hell, and in her dream, Alex had known, without question, that she'd be destroyed if she let him take her...

"Ms. Thorpe?"

Alex swung around.

"Luisa." She gave a choked laugh. "You, ah, you startled me."

"I'm sorry. I only came to see if you were done with your breakfast." Luisa's lips thinned. "I've cleaned up my kitchen but I'd like to tidy up out here, if it's all the same to you."

"Don't worry about the patio, Luisa. I'll take care of it."

"Oh, no, *señora.* Ms. Thorpe. I could never allow you to—"

"Luisa," Alex said brightly, "how's that sister of yours in—was it Santa Barbara?"

"Why—why yes. She's fine, thank you."

"I'll bet you don't get to see her very often." Alex cleared her throat. "Why don't you take the station wagon and drive up for the weekend?"

The housekeeper stared as if Alex had lost her mind.

"The whole weekend, do you mean?"

"Yes. You could leave right now. Wouldn't you like to do that?"

"Of course. But..."

"But?"

"But in all the years I worked for your father and then for your husband, I never—"

"You don't work for them now," Alex said sharply. She took a deep breath. "Luisa. Take the station wagon and go wherever you like. I'm giving you the weekend off."

A while later, she heard the rumble of the front gates as Luisa drove through them. Alex rose and walked through the garden to the koi pond. Carl had added it, after her father's death. She watched the fat, golden fish swimming back and forth, as they always did, back and forth in their elegant, beautiful, perfect prison...

What on earth was the matter with her this morning?

"Get a grip, Alex," she muttered.

Moving quickly, she collected her breakfast dishes and entered the cool darkness of Thorpe House. The kitchen was pristine; even the coffeepot had been emptied, washed and dried. Alex did the same with her few dishes, then looked at the clock.

Could it really be only eight-thirty?

Well, that was fine. She could weed the garden. Carlos would probably scowl on Monday, when he saw she'd invaded his territory but this was *her* house, her kitchen, her life...

The door chimes rang. Alex froze, remembering her dream, and then she laughed. Black Knights didn't ride up to the castle doors and politely ring the bell. Besides, no one could get through the gates without a key.

Luisa must have forgotten something.

She hurried through the entry hall, the stones cold against her bare feet. She smoothed down the skirt of her long white nightgown, undid the bolt and opened the door.

"Luisa," she said, smiling, "what did you..."

Oh! Alex slammed the door shut and fell back against it. It wasn't her sour-faced housekeeper who stood on the steps, it was Travis Baron.

Bang!

"Alex?" The door jolted under the blow of his fist. "Alex, open this door!"

Alex stumbled away from the door, her eyes fixed on it. How had he found her? He didn't know where she lived. She'd never told him...

Bang! Bang!

"Open it, Alex, or so help me God, I'll kick it in!"

A whimper broke from her throat. She thought of the dream, of the Black Knight, and she began to tremble.

"Go away," she said, but the words came out a terrified whisper, lost under the sounds of Travis's fists beating against the door and the answering *thud-thud* of her own heart.

The door shuddered. She'd never thrown the bolt. She was afraid to go back and do it, now. What if the door flew open while she was just behind it? He'd be able to catch her, catch her and—and—

She blanked the terrible thought from her mind. Run, she told herself, run quickly and hide...

But it was too late. The door burst open, and Travis stepped inside.

Alex stared at him, transfixed, not believing what she saw. He was dressed all in black. A black T-shirt fit snugly across his broad shoulders and chest. Faded black jeans clung to his narrow hips and long legs. Black boots, dusty with use, peeked from under the jeans.

He looked wild, and dangerous, and magnificently male. He was not a dream. He was flesh and blood, and he had come for her.

He had come for her.

Terror danced along her spine. Terror...and something else.

His eyes met hers. "Alex," he said softly.

Be calm, she told herself. It was a dream, just a dream. Whatever else Travis Baron might be, he was a civilized man. And she was a civilized woman, who knew how to deal with uninvited guests.

Alex drew herself up. "You're not welcome here, Mr. Baron."

Travis laughed. He'd imagined a dozen scenarios on the way here but not one of them had featured Alexandra Thorpe in a virginal-looking nightgown, standing in the center of a room that looked as if it came straight out of the fifteenth century, facing him down as if he were nothing more than an unwelcome guest when she had to know what had brought him here.

Oh, yes, she knew. He could see it in the darkness of her eyes. In the leap of her pulse, just visible in the hollow of her throat. And in the tension that hummed between them, like electricity through a high-voltage line.

Travis smiled lazily and kicked the door shut. "Is that any way to welcome the man you're supposed to spend the weekend with, Princess?"

Run, the voice inside her said again, run!

But she couldn't. She knew better than to turn her back on a hungry beast, and that was what the man lounging against the door with such seeming carelessness reminded her of, not a Black Knight but a black jaguar, a hungry black jaguar on the prowl that would spring at her, devour her in a heartbeat, if she showed him her fear.

"Don't be ridiculous, Mr. Baron. I never had any intention of spending the weekend with you. Surely, you know that."

"What did you intend to do with me, then, Princess?"

"Nothing," she said quickly. "It was—that was for charity."

He laughed. "Charity, huh?" A smile, as cold and feral as any she'd ever seen, twisted across his mouth. "That's a charming sentiment, Princess. But I'm not in a charitable frame of mind this morning."

"Just—just stop right there, Mr. Baron." Alex swallowed hard as he started slowly toward her. "I swear, if you come any closer, I'll—"

"All that time," he said roughly, "everything that we did, and you still won't call me by my name."

Alex's throat constricted. She took a step back, then another and another. There was a heavy oak chair somewhere behind her; she put out a hand, felt for it and moved around it.

"Mr. Baron—"

Travis kicked the chair aside. Alex danced backward.

"Mr. Baron. I don't know why you came here, sir, but—"

"Don't you?"

God, he was still coming! Still coming...

"Luisa! Luisa? Call the police."

His smile was, she thought, almost gentle. "Luisa?"

"My housekeeper. Yes. Luisa! Dial 9-1-1. Tell them there's an intruder. Tell them—"

"The lady driving the Volvo station wagon? The one who's probably halfway to the valley by now? You ought to tell her to be more careful about locking that gate, Princess."

"My—my chauffeur, then." Alex's voice quavered. "You don't want me to call him. He's—he's big. Very big. He's—he's a former wrestler. And he'll—"

"Call him, by all means. I used to wrassle steers. It's what us cowboys do for fun." Travis flashed a tight grin. "Call your chauffeur, if you've really got one." His eyes turned from green to black as he closed the distance between them. "It won't stop what's going to happen, Alex."

She took another step back. Her shoulders hit the tapestried wall.

"Travis," she said breathlessly, while a honeyed sweetness spread through her.

"Say it again."

Alex swallowed dryly. "Travis. Please..."

"You said that last night, too."

"Said what?" He was inches away from her now, so close that she could feel the heat of his body, smell the mingled scents of sea and soap and, under it all, another smell, one that was wild and primitive and made her pulse quicken. "The only thing I remember saying last night was that I never wanted to see you ag—"

"You said, 'please.'" Desire thickened his voice. "Please, you said, when we were in that doorway, when we were making love."

"It wasn't love! It was—"

"Sex." He reached out and touched his hand to her cheek. His fingertips were rough and callused but his touch was gentle. She imagined herself turning her head, catching his fingers and sucking them into her mouth. The thought left her breathless. "That's fine, Princess. I don't believe in fairy tales that end with forever after."

"And I don't believe in—in rape fantasies."

His quick, dangerous smile turned her bones to jelly. "Neither do I." His thumb rolled over her bottom lip. "I'm talking about a man, and a woman, and what both of them damn well know they want."

"No. Please, Travis, I beg you. If you've any decency at all—"

"Hell, no," he said roughly, "I don't. You pretty much saw to that, last night."

He reached for her. She kicked out, bruised her bare toes on his shin, ducked under his arm and ran. But there was no way to escape him. He caught her halfway across the hall and spun her toward him.

"There's no running away this time, Ms. Thorpe." His tone, and the curl of his fist into the high lace collar of her nightgown, made a mockery of the name. "You're mine, Princess. Or I'm yours. Bought and paid for..."

The fragile cotton tore under his hand. And then, oh then, she was in his arms.

His rage vanished at the touch of her mouth against his. He groaned, threaded his hands into her hair and held her captive to his kiss, but she was a willing prisoner. All that chilly restraint, the memories of her disdain that had kept him pacing the floor most of the night, vanished in a heartbeat.

She was wild in his arms, and what she'd given him last night was nothing compared to what she offered now.

She caught his shirt in her fists, rose on her toes to reach his mouth. He gathered her close, his legs spread so she was cradled against his hardness, and lifted her to him. She moaned; her mouth opened to his and her surrender drove his blood so it thundered in his veins.

She was warm and pliant as silk in his arms; she tasted of sunshine and of flowers. He knew he could take whatever he wanted and he took it all, without mercy. He wanted everything. Her kisses. Her body. Her need.

He touched her. Her breasts. Her belly. The soft golden curls that nestled between her thighs, but none of it was enough. He needed to be inside her, deep inside her, and he couldn't wait for the niceties of a bed or even a carpet. He'd been starving, and she was his feast.

"Travis," she sobbed, "Travis, please..."

The plea, the hunger of it, finished him. He shoved her back against the wall, his hands hard, his need desperate.

"Now," he said, as he unzipped his fly and freed himself.

"Yes. Oh, yes. Oh..."

She cried out as he drove into her. He felt her convulse around him almost instantly, and she cried out, again, shattering herself, shattering him, and he knew that this was only the beginning.

When he could draw breath again, he cupped her face in his hands and kissed her. Then he lifted her into his arms and she clung to his neck, her open mouth pressed to his throat.

He carried her up the wide staircase to a room where the drapes were drawn. And in the artificial twilight of the spring morning, Travis put Alex down in the center of a high, four-poster bed that smelled, as she did, of sunshine and flowers. He undressed and came down on the bed beside her.

He told himself to go slowly this time, to touch her gently and learn all the places that brought her pleasure. He wanted to see her blue eyes turn dark, to watch her shudder with passion. But the sight of her lying beneath him, the tattered remains of her gown spread around her like the torn petals of a flower, her mouth swollen and rosy from his kisses, drove every rational thought from his head.

"Tell me," he demanded, taking her wrists in one hand and stretching her arms high over her head. "Tell me what you want, Princess. I need to hear the words."

He saw the movement of her throat as she swallowed and he knew that even now, after what had happened, she couldn't make the simple admission.

He bent his head and drew the pink tip of her breast into his mouth. She made a soft cry and writhed against him, but he was relentless.

"Say it, Alex."

Her lashes fell to her cheeks. "I can't," she whispered. "Travis, please..."

His free hand drifted down the length of her body and between her thighs.

"Say it," he said, and touched her.

"You," she sobbed, "you, Travis. I want—" A high, keening sound broke from her throat as he entered her. "Yes. Yes. Oh, yes..."

He told himself, again, that he wanted to watch her. And he did, for a moment; he watched as her eyes turned black and bottomless, as her body bowed and arched to his. She lifted her hand and touched his face. It was a gesture that was feminine and strangely gentle in the midst of the whirlwind they rode.

"Travis," she whispered, and touched his face. "Travis..."

Her voice broke, and he was lost. To sensation. To desire. To Alexandra.

Alex came awake slowly and thought, at first, she was deep in her dream.

The hard, warm body pressed against hers. The powerful arm encircling her. The shoulder beneath her cheek...

And then Travis stirred, and murmured something in his sleep, and panic shot through her like an arrow.

What had she done?

Slept with a stranger, Alex, a voice inside said coldly, *that's what you've done.*

She held her breath, afraid that the slightest sound, the faintest motion, would wake him. Carefully, slowly, she eased from the bed.

Her nightgown—what was left of it—lay on the carpet. She burned with embarrassment as she remembered the way he'd torn it in half. The way he'd taken her, against the wall. The way she'd let him take her, let him carry her upstairs and take her again...

Let him, Alex? the voice said slyly.

Images flashed before her eyes. She saw herself wrapping her arms around Travis's neck. Kissing his mouth. Reaching for him, lifting her hips to him as he entered her. Begging him to take her, pleading with him...

A sound trembled in the back of her throat and she whirled around, her fist against her mouth, flew into the bathroom and shut the door behind her.

Shaken, she stood at the sink, head bowed, her hands curled over the white porcelain rim.

The truth was that Travis had taken only what she had been eager to give. She'd wanted him to make love to her, to do everything he'd done. She'd wanted to know what a man like him could make a woman feel...

Could make *her* feel.

Slowly, very slowly, Alex lifted her head and looked into the mirror over the sink.

The sight almost took her breath away.

The woman staring back at her was—was a wanton. It was an old-fashioned word but there wasn't any other way to describe her reflected self. The mass of golden hair, in a mad tangle over her naked shoulders. The eyes, shadowed and deep. The faint blue bruises on her throat and breast. The mouth that was red and—and swollen? Alex touched a fingertip to her lips. Swollen, yes. And tender, from Travis's kisses.

Those kisses. The heat of them. The way he'd parted her lips, entered her mouth with his tongue.

The memory made her tremble. Made her breasts ache. Made her feel hot, and wet.

She swallowed convulsively. What she'd wanted had happened. She wondered now why she'd wanted it. What did it prove, that she could excite a man, or that she could have an orgasm? That she could—color flooded her face—that she could have one with a stranger. With an arrogant, overbearing, dangerous stranger...

"Princess?"

She sprang away from the sink. The doorknob jiggled, and she stared at it as if it were a rattlesnake that had come crawling up from the canyon floor.

"Yes?" Good. Her voice was cool and self-assured. It didn't match the face of the stranger in the mirror, but Travis didn't have to know that. "I, uh, I'm going to shower. There's another bathroom next door that you can—"

The door swung open.

"Showering alone can be dangerous, Alex."

He smiled into her eyes as he clasped her shoulders and looked at her, his gaze slow and steamy as it moved the length of her body. Carl had never looked at her like this. His eyes had never darkened with desire; just watching his face had never made her weak with longing.

"Don't," she whispered, while heat rose in her cheeks.

"Don't what? Look at you?" Travis's eyes met hers. "I want to look at you, Princess. You're the most beautiful woman I've ever seen."

"No." She put her arms over her breasts. "Travis. I'm—I'm—"

Embarrassed. She was embarrassed. The realization stunned him but he knew he was right. It was a long time since he'd seen a woman do anything but preen under a man's admiring gaze but he was seeing embarrassment now. Alex was blushing, and looking down at her toes.

"Princess." Gently, he put his hand under her chin, tilting

her face up to his. "You're beautiful. And I'm the luckiest man in the world, to be able to see you like this."

Her smile trembled. "Really?"

Was her world full of bozos? Or was she searching for compliments? A woman this lovely had to know it.

"Yes. Really."

She smiled again; the shadows seemed to fade from her eyes but there was still a hint of vulnerability in the soft curve of her mouth. Suddenly, he remembered how she'd reacted to some of his kisses and caresses, how she'd cried not only with pleasure but with what might have been surprise at the things he'd done.

He told himself that it was ridiculous to imagine Alexandra Thorpe had found something new in his arms. He'd come into the bathroom wanting her with a hunger their hours of lovemaking had not diminished, imagining what it would be like to take her in the shower, with the water streaming over them.

And he would do that...but not now. Now, something else seemed far more important.

"Travis?" Alex said, as he swung her into his arms.

He silenced her with a kiss.

"Let me show you how beautiful you truly are, Princess," he murmured, and he carried her back to bed, where he kissed her everywhere, savored each sigh and moan. Where he made slow, tender love to her until, at last, she wept with happiness, in his arms.

CHAPTER SIX

HAPPINESS was fleeting.

Alex had known that all her life. But it had never vanished as swiftly as it did now, in the aftermath of Travis's lovemaking.

Her heartbeat slowed. Joy was replaced by despair, and despair by disgust.

She'd just shared endless acts of incredible intimacy with a man she didn't know. What was there to be happy about?

Yes, Travis had made her feel things. His touch had been—it had been everything she'd ever let herself dream a lover's touch might be. Passionate yet tender. Demanding as well as giving. Exciting. Oh, yes, above all else, exciting.

But the man in whose arms she lay wasn't her lover. He was someone she'd bought. There was no getting around that ugly truth.

How? Alex thought, while self-loathing became panic, how could she have done this? She knew she was an anomaly in this age of sexual awareness. She'd gone to her marriage bed a virgin, eager to experience the passion she'd read about. Instead, she'd found sex with her husband was something to be endured. Not painful, not necessarily unpleasant...it was just that she'd expected ecstasy and experienced nothing.

Sometimes—and she'd always felt the guilt of it—sometimes, even as Carl rose above her, she'd found herself thinking about the next day's chores.

Alex bit back a moan of dismay. And yet, she'd cried out in Travis's arms. Her mind had emptied of everything except awareness of what he was doing, of the feel of his

71

hands and mouth, the hardness of his body, the slow, drug-
ging heat of his kisses.

The kisses of a stranger. Of a man she'd bought.

How? she thought frantically. How could this have happened? Had she gone out of her mind? She was a fastidious
woman. She prided herself on her self-control. She never
acted impulsively or foolishly about anything—especially
men. And yet she'd gone to that auction, bought a stranger
and let him—let him…

It was unbelievable. Her friends teased her mercilessly
about the way she acted when they tried to fix her up with
blind dates.

"For heaven's sake, Alex," they'd say, "it's just a date,
not a lifetime commitment."

And she'd smile and say yes, she knew…and then she'd
ask what the man was like? What were his interests, his
hobbies? Who were his friends? Where did he live? How
did he earn his living? By the time she finally sat down to
dinner with the man, he was as familiar to her as an old
acquaintance.

The man lying beside her now, in this bed of tangled
sheets that smelled of sex, was no old friend. He was an
enigma. She had no idea who his friends were, or what he
did for fun. He could be anything from a used car salesman
to a doctor. Maybe he really was a cowboy. There was that
accent that came and went at will, or so it seemed. And
those boots. And that don't-tread-on-me attitude.

The only certainty was that he was handsome. But his
looks didn't justify what she'd spent the day letting him do
to her.

Who was she trying to fool? She hadn't "let" him do
those things. She'd *wanted* him to do them. She'd done
things, too. Done things, felt things…

At least she knew she wasn't a frigid little rich bitch.

She was a tramp.

She was someone she didn't recognize. A woman without
morals, but that was impossible. She was a decent person.

She supported good causes. She didn't lie, cheat or steal; she never even asked her accountant to fudge on her income taxes.

No, she thought, biting back a hysterical laugh, no, she was an honorable, decent person. All she'd done was buy herself a hunk to sleep with. Except, that wasn't accurate. A flush rose in Alex's cheeks. What she'd been doing with Travis hadn't a damned thing to do with sleeping...

"Princess?"

His voice was soft and husky, tinged with that slow, sexy drawl. She didn't want to open her eyes and look at him. If she didn't—if she didn't, maybe he'd disappear. Just get up, get dressed and go away. Then she could pretend this was just a bad dream.

But that wasn't going to happen. He laced his fingers into her hair, turned her face up to his and kissed her. She offered no response. He brushed her mouth with his again, ran his hand down the length of her body, just as if he had the right to do it.

"Princess, are you all right?"

There was no getting around it. She had to open her eyes, look at Travis—at this stranger in her bed. She had to pretend she wasn't ashamed of herself, pretend she was the kind of woman who had sex with men she picked up all the time.

"Alex?"

She took a mental breath and lifted her lashes. Travis was leaning over her, green eyes still dark with what had just happened between them.

"Hey," he said softly, and smiled. "Hello, there, Princess."

"Hello," seemed the wrong thing to say in response. "I, uh, I have to get up," she said, and gave him a forced smile.

"Uh-huh. In a minute. Let me look at you, first."

"Travis—"

"You truly are a beautiful woman, darlin'. Haven't I convinced you of that?"

She didn't want the words to mean anything but there was something in the tone of his voice, in the way he was looking at her, that made her resolve slip, if only for a second. Then she thought of how often a man like this would murmur such words to a woman. A hundred times a month, probably, to a hundred different women, and the momentary glow she'd felt faded and became just another reason to dislike him and despise herself all the more.

"Thank you," she said politely.

"Thank you?" He grinned. Before she could stop him, he rolled her beneath him again and framed her face in his hands. "Such formality, Princess."

"Travis, really. I'd like to—"

"Get up. I know." He smoothed her hair back from her flushed face. "I'm glad I opened those drapes, Princess. Otherwise, I wouldn't have been able to see just how blue those eyes of yours really are." He drew back a little, just enough so he could see her more clearly. "You're really beautiful, Alexandra."

His voice was husky, his eyes dark. She'd seen him look at her this way often enough now to suspect what he was thinking but it wasn't possible. Not after he'd already made love to her so many times.

He moved. Her breath caught. It *was* possible. He wanted her again. And she—heaven help her, she wanted him, too. Her brain was shrieking "no" but her body was already softening and warming in anticipation of the moment he'd slip deep inside her.

He kissed her throat as he cupped her breast. His teeth closed gently on her flesh as his fingers stroked across her nipple. She could feel it happening, feel herself drifting away.

"Travis..."

"What?"

He moved again and she couldn't help it, she gave a soft moan and lifted her hands, lay them lightly on his narrow hips.

"Travis," she said again, but the word was barely a sigh.

"Yes, darlin'. I hear you. Tell me what you want, Princess. Just say it."

Alex's eyes flew open. That little self-satisfied smile was curling over his lips again. Her heart hardened. He knew exactly the effect he had on her and he was determined to make sure she knew it, too.

Her body went rigid.

"Get up," she said.

She knew her voice was icy. He knew it, too. She could see it in the way that smile dropped from his mouth.

"Darlin', what's the matter?"

"Get—up!" she said, and batted her hands against his shoulders.

His eyes narrowed. Her heartbeat stuttered. She thought, once again, how little she knew about this man, how isolated this house was...

He became still. Then he smiled, a quick show of teeth, and rolled away.

"With pleasure, Ms. Thorpe. Far be it from me to keep a lady in bed when she doesn't want to be there."

If he'd wanted to embarrass her, addressing her so formally when she lay naked beside him, he'd succeeded. She wanted to cringe, grab for the sheet and cover herself from head to toe, but she'd sooner have walked through fire than give him that satisfaction. Instead, she swung her legs to the floor, rose to her feet and strolled across the room as if she walked around naked in front of strange men all the time. She picked up her robe from where it lay, shook it out, slipped it on and tied the sash.

Then she turned to Travis.

He was lying as she'd left him, completely naked. His hands were clasped under his head, his feet were crossed at the ankles. And, she was disconcerted to see, he was still partly aroused.

Cover yourself, she wanted to scream—but she was afraid her voice would tremble and give away the truth, that she knew how little it would take to arouse him fully, to make him want her. All she had to do was go to him, put her hand around him. Or her mouth. She hadn't done that, not ever, but suddenly she wanted—she wanted...

She turned away, made what she knew would be a useless search for her slippers, then swung toward him again.

"I'm sure you'd like to shower," she said.

He didn't answer.

"I think I mentioned it earlier, didn't I? That there's another bathroom just down the hall?"

He didn't speak. He just kept looking at her.

"You'll find soaps, toothbrushes, towels—everything you need, in the drawers under the sink.

"How very thoughtful of you, Ms. Thorpe."

There was a warning edge to his voice but she didn't care. All that mattered was getting him out of here.

"But then, I'm sure all your gentlemen guests tell you that."

His meaning was clear. She considered correcting him and decided it would serve no purpose except to feed his ego, but there was no way to stop the color from creeping up under her skin. She lifted her chin, just enough so he'd know she wasn't intimidated.

"I try to be accommodating, Mr. Baron, if that's what you mean."

He smiled lazily, sat up and rose to his feet. "Oh, yes, Ms. Thorpe," he said. His soft drawl, she noticed, was gone. "You surely do. And you're very good at it. At being— what did you call it? Accommodating."

She knew her color was intensifying, along with the desire to fly across the room, slap his face and tell him—tell him what? That she'd never done anything like this before? That she still didn't believe she'd done it? He'd never believe her.

"Mr. Baron." Alex took a deep breath and tucked her hands into the pockets of her robe. "Mr. Baron, it's been an—an enjoyable day...."

"But it's ended." His teeth flashed in a quick, mirthless grin. "Come on, Ms. Thorpe, don't be shy. Or is it that you're trying to act the part of the perfect hostess, and perfect hostesses never want to have to tell a guest, straight out, that the party's over?"

"Mr. Baron. Really, it's just—it's just..." Her eyes fixed on his. "Do you think you could put some clothes on, please?"

Travis looked down at himself, then at her. "My oh my," he said, eyebrows raised in a parody of amazement, the drawl creeping into his voice again. "However did that happen, I wonder? That I'd be standin' here in your bedroom, naked as a jaybird, while you stood over there all dressed up in a robe—a robe coverin' a body which, until a couple of minutes ago, was every bit as naked as mine?" His voice, and his eyes, turned hard. "Or am I supposed to forget little details like that, *Ms.* Thorpe?"

"You're making this unnecessarily difficult," Alex said calmly, even though her heart was thumping again.

His eyes narrowed. He looked at her for what seemed an eternity and then he gave a sharp laugh, reached for his jeans and pulled them on.

"You're right," he said. He sat down on the edge of the bed and tugged on his boots. "And why in hell should it be?"

Alex swallowed dryly. The balance of power had just shifted but she didn't know how, or why. She watched as Travis stood up, grabbed his black T-shirt and put it on. He turned to the mirror over her dresser, ran his hands through his hair as casually as if he were in his own bedroom, then looked at her and smiled. She thought it was a smile, anyway.

"Here we are, two grown-up people." Still smiling, he zipped his jeans, tucked his thumbs into the belt loops and sauntered toward her. "Both of us well over the age of consent. Isn't that right, Princess?"

She wanted to move back before he reached her. That

smile worried her. So did the way he was moving, like a big cat that knew it had finally cornered its prey. But she'd had enough of being humiliated by Travis Baron to last a lifetime. She was damned if she'd permit him to do it again.

"Yes," she said coolly, keeping her eyes on his. "It's absolutely right. I'm glad you see it that way."

"Why, Princess, what other way *could* I see it?" He came to a stop only inches away, close enough so she had to tip her head back to keep meeting his cold green gaze. "I mean, let's just look at how things stand." His smile tilted and the look in his eyes grew even more stony. "It isn't as if I was payin' a social call, Alex. We both know that. You bought me for a purpose—and I delivered."

She could feel herself beginning to tremble. Don't, she told herself furiously, oh, don't let him see that he's starting to frighten you.

"I damn well did deliver, didn't I, Princess?" Travis's tone changed, became as rock-hard as his eyes. "And now you're tired of playing with the hired help."

"I have—I have a dinner appointment," Alex said, trying for some dignity.

"A dinner appointment." His teeth flashed in a cold smile. "Now, isn't that nice?"

"Yes. And—and my date's coming to pick me up soon. So you'd better—"

"Is that a threat, Princess?" The smile glittered again. He put one hand on the wall beside her head and leaned toward her. "Let me give you some advice, Ms. Thorpe." His voice was low and ominous. "Where I come from, nobody's fool enough to buy a stud horse without first checkin' his pedigree."

"I want you out of my house this minute!"

"Playing this kind of game with a strange man could have turned out to be the worst nightmare you ever had." His voice was silky with malice. He shifted his weight and, despite her best intentions, she stumbled back a step. "You don't know me, or what turns me on. I could have done anything I wanted. Beaten you. Bruised you. Left you lying in a pool of your own blood.''

"You're trying to frighten me. And I don't like it.''

"Oh, I think you do. I think maybe that's what turns *you* on.'' She flinched as he encircled her throat with his hand. Her pulse was racing; she felt it jerk beneath his thumb. ''A little hint of danger. Knowin' that the guy you lure into your bed might as easily finish you as—''

"Get out,'' Alex said furiously, ''just get the hell out of my house!''

"I intend to. I wouldn't want to keep you from your date.'' His gaze dropped to her mouth as he touched his thumb over her bottom lip and slid it along the soft crescent. ''But first, I'm making you a promise.''

The words were softly spoken, touched not with malevolence but with something Alex sensed was far more dangerous, something that made her pulse quicken.

"Travis,'' she said quickly, ''you don't understand—''

"I do, Princess. Oh, I do, believe me.'' His hand slid into her hair, cupped her nape. Gently, inexorably, he tipped her face to his. ''I just want to be sure you understand, as well.''

"Understand what?'' she said in a shaky whisper.

"This,'' he said, and crushed her mouth beneath his.

Alex struggled against him. She told herself that, later, assured herself that she put up some kind of resistance...

It was just that it didn't last.

She moaned, caught the fabric of his shirt in her hands, opened her mouth to his and gave herself up to the kiss. He swept his arms around her and gathered her into his embrace, lifted her into the cradle of his hips, rocked her against his hardness.

It was like being swept up in a firestorm. There was no time to think, no wondering what was right and what was wrong. She was on fire and the flames were burning too hot, too fast, to contain.

Travis's mouth clung to hers as he tore open her robe, dragged it off her shoulders and let it puddle at her feet. He shaped her breasts with his hands, then skimmed his palms down her hips and clasped her bottom. Still kissing her, he lifted her to him again.

"Please," she said brokenly. "Oh, Travis, please…"

It was the way he'd taken her that morning, the way he'd almost taken her last night…and yet, this would be different. For all the swiftness of their desire, all the raw, primal urgency, Alex felt a sweetness to it now. It made her tremble. She'd wanted Travis to teach her what a woman could feel, but she felt more, in his arms. She felt—she felt…

He put her from him so abruptly that she almost fell. Her eyes flew open. She looked at him through the mist of her tears and saw a face that might have been chiseled from granite.

"You see, Princess? You were wrong. Truth is, I could still be of some service to you, if I wanted." He smiled coldly. "You think about that tonight, *Ms.* Thorpe, after you and your 'dinner date' come back here for a round of fun and games. Think about it, and about me, while you're in bed and he's—"

Her fist whirred through the air, connected cleanly with his jaw. Travis was caught off guard. His head jerked back and a spot of blood appeared at the corner of his mouth. Alex gasped for breath as she watched him put his finger to the cut.

"Get out," she whispered hoarsely. "Do you hear me? Get out! Get—"

She looked around wildly, grabbed the only thing near at hand and hurled it at his head but her aim with the lamp wasn't as good as with her fist. It hit the wall and shattered into a score of pieces.

Travis laughed and strolled way. "Have a pleasant evening, Ms. Thorpe," he said, and slammed the door after him.

"Bastard," Alex yelled, "you no good bastard!"

She spun around, grabbed her robe and put it on. Who

did he think he was? Did he really imagine he could treat her this way and get away with it?

She needed—what? A drink. She never drank, she hated the taste of whiskey but by God, a drink was what she needed now, to get the taste of Travis Baron out of her mouth. And then she'd shower.

No. No, first she'd rid the room of any trace of the most despicable man she'd ever known.

She marched to the bed, stripped off the sheets and pillowcases and carried them to the marble fireplace on the other side of the bedroom. She wouldn't sully the hamper with them, or even the washer.

Grimly, she dumped the stuff on the grate and opened the flue.

"Goodbye, Mr. Baron," she said, as she struck a match.

And goodbye to whatever insanity had possessed her to have wanted him in the first place.

The pale blue linens went up in a satisfying blaze. Within minutes, nothing remained but ashes. Alex sat back on her heels. Fire was cleansing. Wasn't that what people said?

Well, she thought, as she closed the fire screen and got to her feet, she felt cleansed.

She stripped off her robe, kicked it into a corner and went into the bathroom.

The only true words Travis had spoken were the ones about her being an adult. She *was* an adult, free to do what she chose, even if what she chose was stupid. She'd done something she'd always regret but there wasn't much sense in brooding over it. Besides, in today's world, having sex with a man you never intended to see again wasn't exactly a crime.

Alex doubled over and clutched the rim of the sink.

What was the sense in pretending? She'd never forgive herself for today. Never. Not for sleeping with Travis, although that was bad enough. What she'd never forgive herself for was still wanting him, at the end. Even after she'd had time to come to her senses, even after the terrible things he'd said, she'd wanted him. If he'd carried her to the bed, she'd have gone willingly. She'd have trembled in his arms again, cried out his name again, done all those things again...

Alex moaned and jammed her fist against her mouth.

Getting Travis Baron out of her bed had turned out to be easy. Getting him out of her head, it seemed, was going to be just a little more difficult.

Halfway along the road that led down through Eagle Canyon, Travis snarled an obscenity, downshifted so abruptly that the gears protested and pulled the Porsche onto the dirt shoulder.

"Dammit to hell," he growled, and slammed the heel of his hand against the steering wheel.

He'd managed to look nonchalant when he'd strolled out of Alex's bedroom but the truth was, his gut was churning the way it had before his first bull ride, twenty years ago. He knew he had to calm down. The road was narrow and curving, with enough blind spots to make even him wary, and he'd been storming along it at a speed he didn't even want to think about. There was no sense in killing himself or, worse still, some other poor soul just because he was so angry at Alex that he could hardly think straight.

One of them was crazy, and it sure wasn't him.

Travis snorted. Who was he kidding? She was nuts, yeah, but so was he. And he didn't like the feeling, not one bit.

A while ago, she'd been like a wildcat in his arms. He'd never known anything like it and the immodest truth was that he was a man who'd known a lot of hot, wild women. But there'd been more to this woman than heat. Her hesitancy, her shy yet eager reactions to everything he'd done and said, had been different from anything he'd ever experienced.

And the last time they'd made love, at the end, she'd cried.

"Did I hurt you, Princess?" he'd whispered.

"No," she'd said, "oh, no."

And she'd clasped his face in her hands, brought his mouth to hers and kissed him with a sweetness that had pierced his heart.

He'd smiled, and kissed her gently. Held her close, until her breathing eased, gone on holding her, looking at her, trying to figure out how he'd gone from wanting nothing more than a primitive act of dominating male vengeance to wanting everything from the beautiful stranger in his arms.

And then she'd opened those eyes of hers, looked at him as if he were a rattlesnake she'd found tucked in the sheets instead of a man, and told him, in no uncertain terms, to get his ass out of her bed, and out of her life.

He could feel the rage still pumping through his body. Never, not once in his entire life, not even when he'd come home and found his wife in bed with her damned tennis pro...not even then had he been so plain-out furious at a woman. Hell, he'd never even imagined a man could *be* this angry at a woman.

Travis turned on the engine.

Okay. Yes. Definitely, the thing to do was to put some distance between Alex Thorpe and him.

Either that or drive back up the road, march into that mausoleum of a house, toss her over his shoulder, carry her back to bed and ride her until that snooty look tumbled from her face, until she arched her back and lifted her hips, wound her arms around his neck the way she had before.

Or he could gather her into his arms, hold her close to him, just hold her, with his face buried in her sweet-smelling hair, her lips against his throat, while the long afternoon turned into night.

Travis's jaw tightened. Man, he was losing it!

He reached for the key, slammed the car into gear and took the Porsche, engine screaming like a banshee, down the canyon road at a speed that would have astonished even him, if he'd been thinking about anything except the insanity of wanting to see Alexandra Thorpe again in this lifetime.

CHAPTER SEVEN

ALMOST two weeks later, Travis slipped off his headset, made sure everything in the cockpit of his Piper Comanche was secure and stepped out on Espada soil for the first time in close to two years.

It was a hot June morning, with the kind of airless and oppressive heat he remembered from his childhood. Insects buzzed and hummed in the grass alongside the parking area, just as they always had, He had the crazy feeling that his father was going to ride into view, look at him from under his bushy brows and say, "Boy, why're you here, lazin' around, instead of at the barns, doin' your chores?"

He wasn't in the mood for this, not for the old memories or for dealing with Jonas, or for being polite to the couple of hundred guests who were sure to be here by this time tomorrow. It seemed he hadn't been able to be polite to anybody lately. Even the guys at his office were steering clear of him, ever since he'd almost knocked Pete Haskell on his butt the Monday after the auction.

"Hey, Baron," Haskell said, "how'd it go with the Thorpe babe?"

"It went fine."

Travis's response had been clipped. Any intelligent man would have seen it as a warning and backed off, but nobody had ever credited Pete with a surplus of intelligence.

"It went fine," Pete had mimicked, with a leer. "Details, Baron. We want details. Is she as hot as she looks? Did you get into her pants?"

Travis had shoved him, none too gently, against the wall, which was pretty stupid considering that getting into Alex's pants was exactly what he'd wanted—and what he'd done.

"Watch your mouth," he'd snarled at Pete, after two of the other partners had pulled him back.

Nobody much had bothered with him since, and that was fine. He knew he was grumpy but hell, it had nothing to do with Alexandra Thorpe. He was busy, that was all. A corporate merger gone bad and a liability suit against another client looked as if it was headed for a jury trial. He was overworked, was all.

His bad mood didn't have a damned thing to do with Alex Thorpe...

"Cut the crap, Baron," Travis muttered.

It had everything to do with her, and why wouldn't it? No man wanted to be dismissed, the way he had. His mood was foul and spending a weekend with Jonas was not going to improve it.

Travis turned on his heel and looked at the Comanche. Nobody knew he'd arrived. All he had to do was climb into the plane, head west to the coast...

A hand clamped down on his shoulder.

"Do it," a familiar voice growled, "and I swear, I'll hunt you down and take that empty head of yours for a trophy."

Travis turned around and looked into the smiling face of his brother, Slade.

"You into mind-reading now, kid?"

"Not unless you expect me to believe you have a mind to read, big brother."

Travis glowered. Slade went right on smiling.

"Oh, hell," Travis said, after a few seconds, and he grinned and threw his arms around his brother. "Can't get away with a thing when you're around." He stepped back and looked Slade over. "Still ugly as ever, I see."

Slade eyed him back, taking in the dark gray trousers, white-on-white shirt complete with maroon silk tie dangling from the open neck and grinned.

"Yup. It must run in the family."

Travis laughed, reached into the plane and began unloading his things. "Gage hasn't changed his mind again, has he? He's still coming, right?"

"Yeah, he'll be here. Jeez, man, what'd you do? Bring along your whole office?"

"Some of us know what it means to put in a day's work, kid," Travis said as he handed over his jacket, briefcase and computer. "I came to this oven straight from a meeting."

"Now he's gonna name-drop," Slade said, rolling his eyes skyward. "Go on, drop those Hollywood names all over the place. See if it means anything to me that you're up to your kneecaps in blond bimbettes just achin' to demonstrate their talents in your bed."

"I am not up to anything in blondes," Travis said sharply.

Slade's eyebrows rose. "Okay. Whatever you say."

"And why'd you make that crack, anyway?"

"Hey, man, it was just a—"

"Not all blondes are bimbettes. And not every woman who comes onto a man is—is…" His voice faded away. "Holy hell," he muttered.

"Uh, Trav? Did I put my foot into a cow pie just now, or something?"

"Or something," Travis said, after a second. He laughed, or tried to. "It's the heat. This darned Texas heat. I'm just not used to it anymore."

"Uh-huh."

"It's like an oven."

"You already said that."

"Well, I'm saying it again. Dammit, Slade—"

"Dammit, Travis, why are you so busy tryin' to change the subject?"

"What subject?"

"The subject of why you almost took my head off just now?"

The brothers had reached the Jeep Slade had left parked on the grass. They paused on opposite sides of the vehicle and looked at each other across its roof.

It would be so easy to tell him, Travis thought. To just say, "You remember that auction? And the blonde I told you about? Well, I spent the day in bed with her. And yeah, I'm too old to think babes like that are worth a man's time but the thing is, see, I keep thinking about her, and remembering little things that don't add up. Like the way she turned cold and threw me out, though she'd cried, that last time she came in my arms..."

"Trav?"

Travis blinked. Slade was staring at him with a worried look on his face. What was he going to do? Make the look permanent by telling him stuff not even he, himself, could understand? No way, he thought, and forced a smile to his lips.

"You know what I need, kid?"

"No. And, apparently, neither do you."

Travis grinned and tossed his things into the Jeep. "I need a shower. A change of clothes. A bottle of beer and a maybe a swim down at the old creek."

Slade grinned back at him. "I thought you Hollywood types were into vintage vino?"

"You know what they say, my man. When in Rome..."

"...drink Texas Red. Make that two bottles, icy-cold, and you're on."

Travis smiled and offered his hand. Slade clasped it in the intricate, secret Los Lobos handshake of their childhood.

"We're lean," Travis said.

Slade smiled. "We're mean."

"We're part of the team," they said in unison.

Laughing, they climbed into the Jeep and sped toward the house.

The shower and the change of clothes helped. So did the first beer.

An hour after that, seated on the deck and watching a pair of tiny hummingbirds fight a duel over bragging rights to a patch of honeysuckle, Travis had just about decided this weekend in the country might do him some good, after all.

Slade had gone back into the house to collect another couple of cold beers. All was almost right with the world. Now, if only Catie would show up...

"Travis!"

He looked up, grinned and got to his feet in time to catch his stepsister in his arms and whirl her around.

"Hey, darlin'," he said, kissing her soundly on each cheek, "I was starting to wonder if you'd decided to ditch this whole party thing."

Caitlin wrinkled her nose. "Fat chance, considering that it was my idea."

"With a little prompting from Jonas, huh?"

She smiled. "Well, maybe just a little. When did you get in?"

"An hour ago." He pulled a long face. "I was pretty disappointed that you weren't part of the welcoming committee."

"I wanted to be, but—"

"Catie, I'm only teasing you." Travis grinned. "Slade was there. What more could a man possibly want?"

Caitlin laughed as she plopped into a rocker and stretched out her denim-clad legs, "True, but I really was going to be down at the landing strip. Then Jonas decided somebody ought to drive into town and check up on the caterer, so—"

"So he told you to take care of it."

"Now, Trav, don't be like that. That's just the way he is, and you know it."

Travis sat down in a high-backed wicker chair. "Yeah. Some things never change."

"Have you seen him yet?"

"No. Marta says he's out riding." He smiled. "She looks terrific."

"She *is* terrific." Caitlin kicked back her rocker. "Amazing, isn't it? No matter what he does, Jonas can't scare her off."

A companionable silence fell over the porch, broken only by the squeak of the rocking chair and the hum of the bees in the flowers. After a while, Travis cleared his throat.

"So, what's the deal, Catie? Are we here to wish Jonas another eighty-five years as emperor, or to listen to him tell Slade and Gage and me that we should be fighting over which of us gets to inherit this place not one of us would know what to do with. You'd think he'd get it into his thick head that you're the only one who wants Espada."

"But I'm not one of you," Caitlin said softly. "You're Barons. I'm a McCord."

"Bull-spit."

"Not according to your father." Caitlin reached for Travis's beer, lifted it to her lips and took a long drink. "I do think that's on the agenda, though," she said, rolling the icy bottle across her forehead. "Jonas's attorney is coming down."

"His attorney, huh?"

"Uh-huh. Grant Landon, from New York."

"Landon." Travis cocked an eyebrow. "Don't think I've heard of him but I don't suppose I would have, out in L.A."

Caitlin smiled. "Speaking of L.A., what's new in your life?"

The door slammed as Slade stepped onto the deck, two long-necked beer bottles dangling from each hand.

"Hell, Catie, don't encourage him." He put the bottles on the floor and settled his long frame into one of the wicker chairs. "You show the least bit of interest, old Travis is gonna deluge us with fancy stories about the Hollywood high life."

"Deluge me, Trav," Caitlin said. "Sometimes, I forget there's more to the world than calving and roping."

"With pleasure." Travis reached for her hand, curled it into his and brought it to his lips. "Did you know that there's not a Hollywood actress as beautiful as you?"

"Liar," Catie said, and smiled.

"And there sure as heck isn't a big-time Hollywood

heartthrob anywhere near as good-lookin' as any your big brother Travis.''

Catie chortled with laughter. The sound sent a pleasant warmth rolling through Travis's blood.

Jonas or no Jonas, he thought, it was good to be home.

He met Jonas's attorney during an impromptu meeting in the hayloft, which had always been the secret Los Lobos clubhouse.

And what a hell of a meeting it had been, Travis thought grimly, as he dressed for his father's birthday party.

There they were, the three Baron brothers, he and Slade still reeling over Gage's admission that he and Natalie had split up, and along had come Grant Landon to admit he was facing the same trouble with his wife.

The only certainty in relationships between the sexes, Travis thought as he looked in the mirror and adjusted his bow tie, was that there were no certainties in relationships between the sexes. That had been the general consensus that had come out of the impromptu Los Lobos meeting.

Travis sighed and put the studs through his cuffs.

When they were growing up, a Los Lobos meeting meant talk about baseball, or football, or maybe secret plans to sneak out of their rooms at midnight to look for whatever trouble a trio of kids could get into on a ranch the size of a small country.

This time, it had been all about women. Gage's bewilderment at his wife's decision to leave him. Grant Landon's dismay at his wife telling him she was unhappy. Slade hadn't said much but he'd had a funny look about him, as if he could have contributed a lot to the discussion, if he'd wanted to.

Landon had dubbed it a meeting of The I Don't Understand The Female Of The Species Club which, come to think of it, had been pretty close. Travis had just kept silent. What could he have said about feeling anger for a woman he hardly knew that would have made sense?

Anger, and lust.

His eyebrows drew together over his slightly bent nose.

How could you be so angry at a woman and still want her so badly it made you ache? Because he did still want her. If he went down the stairs tonight and, by some stroke of fate, found Alex in the crowd milling through the house...if that happened, he'd go straight to where she stood, take her in his arms, shake her until her teeth rattled and then—and then...

"You're an idiot, Baron," Travis said to his glowering reflection.

Why would he want a woman like her? He didn't like teases. And he sure didn't like being used. Equality of the sexes was fine but what Alex had done to him was role reversal in spades. Wham, bam, thank you—sir.

Even he had never been guilty of that. He'd never taken a woman to bed and then just unceremoniously dumped her. He dated her for a while, took her to dinner, whatever. And, when the affair ran its course, he sent flowers, an expensive little gift...

Travis laughed.

"Hell, pal," he said to his image, "is that what this is all about? Would you feel better if the lady had sent you a couple of dozen roses and a Tiffany tie clasp?"

The tension eased from his shoulders.

He'd been acting like a jerk, and now he knew the reason. Alex Thorpe had dented his ego.

"That is pathetic," he said to the guy in the mirror, and grinned.

He slipped into the jacket to his tux, then ran his hands through his hair. He could hear music and laughter drifting from the garden. The party had started. Two hundred guests, Catie had told him, and then she'd smiled in that cute way of hers and said that she'd fielded a dozen phone calls from girls he'd grown up with, wanting to know if he'd be in attendance.

"I swear, Trav," she'd said, waggling her eyebrows, "I don't know how you're going to handle 'em all."

Travis gave himself one last look in the mirror. "Yeah," he said solemnly, "it's gonna be tough. But somebody's got to do it."

He grinned. Then, whistling cheerfully through his teeth, he left his room and went down the stairs to join the party.

A couple of hours later, he stood in the living room, a flute of Dom Perignon in one hand and a lobster canapé in the other.

The wine was great and so were the hors d'oeuvres. The band was terrific, whether it was playing rock, Texas two-steps or stuff that was soft and dreamy. And, as Catie had promised, lots of his old conquests were there, all of them still gorgeous and most of them making it clear they were still interested, even some of the ones who had a husband or boyfriend in tow. In fact, there were lots of stunning women on hand, including a model whose face had adorned enough covers so even he recognized her, and the daughter of a senator who was even more beautiful in person than she was in her father's campaign ads.

He'd danced with them all, flirted with the unattached ones, and the cover girl's phone number, along with that of the senator's daughter, were safely tucked into his breast pocket.

"Having fun?" Catie called, as she danced by in the arms of Travis's cousin, Leighton.

"Oh, sure," he said heartily.

Too heartily. He knew it as soon as he spoke, but Leighton was bending Catie's ear, probably going on and on about himself the way he always did, so Travis got away with the lie. Jonas and Marta, however, weren't so easy to fool, when he went over to pay his respects a few minutes later.

Marta, elegant as always, leaned forward and kissed his cheek.

"You're the most handsome man in the room," she said. "Are you having a good time?"

"Yes, of course." Travis smiled at his stepmother. "It's a wonderful party."

"Will ya listen to this?" Jonas said. "The two of you are so busy lyin' to each other, it's enough to make my stomach turn."

Marta raised her eyebrows. "Excuse me?"

"Here's my wife, sayin' my son's the best-lookin' man around, when everybody knows the sleekest stallion at this here party is me."

Marta laughed. Travis managed to smile.

"And here's my son, sayin' what a dandy party this is when all it takes is one look at him to know he's just countin' the minutes till he can get his so-phis-to-cated tail away from here and hurry back to the bright lights of Holly*wood*. Ain't that right, boy?"

Marta put her hand on her husband's arm. "Now, Jonas…"

"You're right, as usual, Father," Travis said pleasantly, "except for one thing. I stopped being a boy years ago."

"So you keep tellin' me. But I sure ain't seen no proof of it yet."

Travis put his empty wineglass on the tray held by a passing waiter.

"As always, Father, talking with you has been a pleasure." He took Marta's hand and kissed it. "Marta."

"Oh," she said gently, "Travis, please don't leave."

"He ain't leavin'. I need to have a little talk with him first."

"We've had our talk. Now, if you'll excuse me—"

"Got a job I need you to do for me, boy." The old man's hard mouth curled. "Tra-vis, I mean," he said, exaggerating the name.

"What job? Break a mustang that's already sent one of the hands to the hospital? Spend the night camped in a meadow where a mountain lion's been sighted, track it down and kill it by myself, just to prove I'm a man?'' Travis smiled with his teeth. "Sorry, Father, I went that route twenty years ago."

"You're the eldest son I got, Travis. Those was things you needed to do."

"Yeah, well, I did them. And I'm not interested in doing anything more for—"

"'Course, you'd have to spend a little time out of that there Holly*wood* to do it."

"Sounds fascinating," Travis said politely. "But I'm not interested."

"This is a fancy-pants job. One that re-quires that law degree of yours and that la-di-da attitude you got about that stuff you're drinkin'."

Jonas? Wanting to use his knowledge of law as well as wine, without making it sound as if neither was masculine? It was almost enough to make Travis change his mind...

"Unless, of course, you ain't a good enough lawyer to take on somethin' for me."

Travis smiled. "Happy Birthday, Father," he said, and strolled away.

He danced some more. Flirted some more. Drank some more of the memorable champagne and discovered that the senator's daughter kissed with her mouth open. And, as he moved slowly around the dance floor with the model's lush body pressed to his, Travis came to two conclusions.

The first was that the model's incredible breasts were almost definitely her own, the second that he'd been a fool to have wasted so much time, thinking about Alex. How wrong he'd been, earlier tonight, thinking he'd have gone straight to her if, by some quirk of fate, she were in this crowd...

Until he looked across the room and saw a slender blonde with silky hair and endless legs standing with a man's arm encircling her waist. Her back was to him but he could tell she was laughing by the tilt of her head and by the look on the man's face.

"Excuse me," he said to the model, and left her in the

middle of the dance floor. He strode across the room, grasped the blonde's arm and turned her toward him.

"Alex," he said…except, it wasn't Alex. It was a pretty woman with blue eyes and blond hair but it wasn't the woman he'd spent the past two weeks wanting.

Travis apologized. He smiled charmingly. And he set off to find his father.

Jonas was in the library, holding court, surrounded by a half a dozen or so men. It was, Travis thought dryly, a Who's Who in the world of power and leadership. The room smelled of pricey bourbon, Cuban cigars and expensive cologne.

Jonas looked up as Travis entered the room. "Travis."

Travis nodded. "Father."

The man most likely to be the next president of the United States waved his glass.

"Anyway, as I was saying…"

"Say it later," Jonas said.

There was a silence. Then the man who would be president cleared his throat. "You know," he said briskly, "I've been dying to taste some of that Texas barbecue."

The room emptied. Jonas walked slowly across the hand-woven Navajo rug and closed the door.

"I take it you haven't come to tell me again that your childhood was an all-fired disaster," he said.

"I never did tell you. What would have been the point?" Travis walked to the mahogany sideboard that dominated one wall, opened a bottle of mineral water and poured it, over ice, into a crystal tumbler. "What's this job you have for me?"

Jonas smiled. "Thought you wasn't interested."

"I might not be." Travis drank some of the water, put down the glass and folded his arms. "But you said it would take me out of L.A. for a while and I'm in the mood for a change of scene. I figured I'd at least listen to the details."

Jonas folded his arms, too, and leaned back against the

wall. Amazing, Travis thought. The old man was eighty-five, but he still looked as hard and wiry as ever.

"Never mind all that politeness crap you gave Marta," Jonas said. "You're not havin' much fun tonight, are you?"

"No," Travis said bluntly, "I'm not." A tight smile flickered across his mouth. "But you can't take any credit for it."

His father laughed. "Woman trouble."

"What makes you think so?"

Jonas strolled to the sideboard and poured two fingers of bourbon into his glass.

"Saw you outside with that brunette a while ago. The senator's girl." The old man tossed back half the bourbon. "Looked like she was tryin' to swallow your tongue. Am I right?"

Travis couldn't help laughing. "I'm sure there's a more romantic way to put it, Father, but yes, that's pretty accurate."

"And you was about as interested as a stallion would be in a cow."

"Father, your perceptions of my love life are all very interesting, but—"

"Sex life, Boy. Don't you make none of those stupid mistakes about love. What a man feels for a woman comes straight from his crotch. Mess it up with love, that's where the problems start."

Travis looked at the bottle of bourbon, sighed, drank down his water and poured some into his glass.

"I'm sure Marta would be delighted to hear that," he said.

"I'm not saying I don't care for Marta. I do. But a man who lets himself think he's in love is a man in trouble."

Travis looked at his father. The old man was staring into the distance. His voice had lost its lazy Texas drawl, and gone flat.

"You sound as if you're speaking from experience," Travis said softly.

Jonas went on staring for another couple of seconds. Then he took a deep breath, rolled his shoulders and laughed.

"Man gets to be my age, he's seen enough to know you don't have to be a jackass to recognize one."

Travis sipped at his bourbon. "You going to get around to telling me what this job is you'd like me to handle for you?"

His father eased into his favorite leather armchair. His motions were fluid but slower than they'd once been. He really was getting old, Travis thought suddenly. To his surprise, he felt an unexpected twinge of compassion.

"Here's the situation." Jonas sat back and crossed his feet at the ankles. "I got me a deal in the works. A company I want to buy, in your neck of the woods. Well, your neck of the woods, figuratively speakin'. It's up in the Napa Valley."

"That's wine country, Father."

Jonas chuckled. "And a good thing it is, considerin' that the company I'm lookin' at makes wine."

"You? Buying a vineyard?"

"Baron money is invested in lots of things, Travis. If you paid more attention, you'd know that."

Travis sat down opposite Jonas and told himself not to respond to the taunt.

"If you just want some contracts checked out, I know a couple of guys in Northern California I can recommend."

"You're supposed to know somethin' about wine, isn't that right, boy?"

"I know enough about it to know what I like to drink and don't like, but if you're thinking I know anything about vineyards—"

"I got me a bunch of business managers but not a one of 'em I'd trust to tell a Zinfandel from a Beaujolais." Jonas smiled. "What's wrong, son? You look as if you jes' stepped on a fire ant."

"Nothing," Travis said evenly, "except that I'm amazed to hear those two words rolling off your tongue."

Jonas rose from his chair, went to the sideboard and poured another inch of bourbon into his glass.

"I'd need you to go up there for a day. Two, at the most."

"And do what? Knowing a Zin from a Beaujolais comes in handy when you're reading a wine list, but it doesn't have a damned thing to do with checking out a contract."

"It is, if you take along my peoples' financial reports, and if you put to use some of that stuff you know about oak barrel curing, viniculture..." Jonas chuckled. "There's that look on your face again, boy."

Travis laughed. He didn't mean to but hell, he couldn't help it.

"You're still a surprise to me, Father," he said.

"Life's full of surprises, boy. Well? Will you do it, or won't you?"

Travis thought about it. A couple of days up north, five hundred miles away from Malibu, and Los Angeles. It sounded pretty good. He liked the Napa Valley; he'd spent some weekends there. And, yeah, he did know a lot about viniculture. There was a time he'd considered sinking some money into a winery.

And then there was Alexandra Thorpe, and getting her out of his head.

"Yes," he said, before he could think about it too long and change his mind. He put down his glass and held out his hand. "I'll be glad to do it, Father. Just get together all those reports you mentioned and have them sent to me."

Jonas's hand closed on Travis's. "Already did," he said, and grinned. "Figured you wouldn't be able to pass up a chance like this, seein' as how you fancy yourself a hotshot lawyer and an expert on wine."

"Seein' as how you figure yourself an expert on how I'd react to your offer, you mean," Travis said, with a lazy smile.

"Somethin' like that." The old man drank the last of his bourbon, put down his glass and dug his hands into the pockets of his tux. "Anythin' else you need, you jes let me know."

Travis nodded and started from the room. At the last second, he swung toward Jonas.

"The vineyard."

"What about it?"

"Maybe I'm already familiar with it, Father. What's its name?"

Jonas frowned. "Hawk's Nest. Eagle's Nest. Somethin' like that." He strode to his desk, opened a drawer and rifled through some papers. "Here it is. Peregrine Vineyards. Used to be run by somebody didn't know a thing about wine, guy name of, lemme see here... Stuart. Carl Stuart."

Travis shrugged. "Never heard of him."

"Place actually belonged to his wife. Still does, now that she's divorced. She's gone back to usin' her maiden name. Got it right here, someplace."

"It doesn't matter," Travis said, his hand on the doorknob. "I don't know the name of the vineyard, so I doubt if I'd know the name of—"

"Here it is." Jonas looked up. "Lady's name is Thorpe. Alexandra Thorpe."

Travis felt the floor tilt under his feet. "Alexandra Thorpe?" he said hoarsely.

"Uh-huh." His father gave him a slow smile. "Is that a problem, boy?"

Their eyes met. Travis thought about asking what the old man knew, about how he could possibly know it...

And then he thought of the woman who'd haunted him ever since he'd walked out of Thorpe House two weeks ago, and about putting an end to this nonsense, once and for all.

"No," he said calmly, "it isn't a problem. Not in the slightest."

CHAPTER EIGHT

ALEX had known people would whisper about the auction.

She also knew that no one would dare say anything to her face. What was said behind her back didn't matter. Let the gossips speculate to their souls' damnation. She would pay no attention.

No, she thought, as she walked along a row of grapes at Peregrine Vineyards, the whispers about that night didn't bother her.

But the dreams did.

She dreamed about Travis Baron. Erotic dreams, the kind that left the sheets twisted between her thighs. Sometimes she awakened flushed with heat, the all-too-real feel of Travis's kisses on her mouth. Even thinking about it now made her bones feel as soft as the pulp of the grapes in the fermenting vats.

She had other dreams, too. Tender ones, of Travis holding her in his arms, just holding her, nothing more. Or dancing with her, in a flower-filled garden, his kisses as soft as the whisper of the breeze. The dreams were silly; she knew that. They were half-remembered perfume commercials, playing in her head. Grown women did not have such girlish, romanticized flights of imagination.

High overhead, a hawk cried out its pleasure as it soared toward the sun on a thermal current of hot valley air. Alex tilted her head back, looked up and wondered what it felt like to be so free. She had never been free, not of the responsibility to live the life first her father, and then her husband, had laid out for her. And it had seemed enough, until that Friday evening, two weeks ago, when she'd gone into the exciting embrace of a stranger.

It had taken her a while to understand why she was wasting her time thinking about a man who didn't deserve it but, finally, she did. It was because she didn't have enough to keep her busy.

The idea—that there was more to life than the things that filled hers—had actually been perking for a while.

She'd never really thought about the way she lived before. She'd been raised to be an obedient daughter in the expectation that she'd marry someone in the same circle of people she'd known all her life, and that she'd be an excellent hostess and a good wife to him. She was an expert at making half an hour's worth of polite conversation about absolutely nothing and planning an elegant meal for ten or two hundred. She'd never questioned her role: she'd deferred first to her father's wishes and then to her husband's. She'd hated her marriage but she'd probably have stayed in it, if she hadn't returned home one day and found Carl in her bedroom with another woman.

Oh, yes. Until two weeks ago, she'd played her role impeccably.

Alex paused and scuffed her bare toes in the cool, sandy soil.

Her father would have turned purple at the sight of her walking around this way. Carl, too. It isn't suitable, they'd have said, but their shock would have been nothing compared to that of her attorneys and business manager when she'd refused to simply sign away Peregrine Vineyards without first meeting the prospective buyer, even though the vineyard had been for sale for several months without so much as an offer.

Her business manager had looked vaguely alarmed. "Surely, you're not having second thoughts about selling Peregrine? We've explained how much money it would take to make the vineyard profitable, Ms. Thorpe, and that we are convinced it's not worth the investment."

"You have. And I still wish to sell. But I want to meet the buyer."

"Whatever for?" one of the lawyers had asked.

She thought about telling them that she'd decided to take a greater interest in the workings of her inherited estates but from the looks on their faces, she'd decided it might be best to leave that news for another day. Instead, she'd told them that she had a special fondness for Peregrine, which was true enough.

She'd seen the winery years before, when she'd inherited it. Carl had taken her to the Napa Valley for what she'd foolishly thought was a romantic getaway weekend but had only been his way of checking out the property. Her disappointment had been minimal; by then, she'd known not to expect much from her marriage. What had surprised her was that she'd fallen in love with Peregrine on sight. The acres of grapevines, the gently rolling hills, the big Victorian farmhouse standing on a grassy rise...

"It's beautiful," she'd said, and then added, impulsively, "Why don't we fix up the house and use it for weekends?"

"Don't be foolish, Alex," Carl had replied brusquely. "Peregrine isn't a toy, it's a business venture."

He was right, of course. That was why she was selling it. Alex sighed, tucked her hands into the pockets of her linen trousers and began walking. Okay, maybe it was silly but she didn't want to hand Peregrine over to a faceless entity. It was why she'd insisted on a meeting.

"But it isn't done," her senior attorney had said, the same way she imagined he'd have said, "My God, Ms. Thorpe, there's an alligator swimming in your bathtub."

"Why isn't it?" Alex had replied politely, and the men had rushed in with explanations that ranged from the logical to the absurd, but it had all come down to the same thing.

Her father would not have permitted it, and neither would Carl.

"My father is dead," Alex had said. "And Carl Stuart is no longer my husband."

And so, here she was, walking the dusty rows of the vineyards, looking at the grapevines as if she knew something

about them when she didn't know anything, heading toward
the Victorian farmhouse for a meeting with a man who'd
probably been told he'd have to endure fifteen minutes of
idiotic fluff, if he wanted the purchase to go through.

Alex paused at the end of the row of grapevines, where
she'd left her shoes, and put them on. She didn't know why,
but she felt uncertain. It was a new feeling, and she didn't
like it. She'd felt this way only once before, after she'd bid
on Travis.

She frowned, straightened her shoulders and walked up
the rise. This was not the time to let her thoughts wander.
She'd never see Travis again. What she had to concentrate
on now was the man waiting for her at the house.

What would she say to him? What would she ask? She
didn't even know his name, or his function. In her deter-
mination to face down her advisor and her attorneys, she'd
forgotten to ask them any of the things she should have. He
represented the buyer. That was all she knew.

One of her lawyers would be present at this meeting, of
course, but she didn't want to let him do all the talking. She
wanted to participate. She was a good judge of people; she
could ask questions that would give her some insight into
this unknown buyer's intentions because, silly or not, she
wanted Peregrine to have the best possible stewardship.

Alex smoothed back her hair. The breeze had teased the
strands loose from the knot her hairdresser had secured at
her nape this morning. Glancing down, she saw that her
toes, exposed in her Italian sandals, were faintly gritty from
her walk.

"A good beginning, Alex," she muttered—and came to
a dead stop.

There was a car in the driveway, parked alongside her
rented sedan. Her attorney drove a black Cadillac and this
car was black. But it was a Porsche. Her heart banged
against her ribs. Travis drove a black Porsche.

Alex laughed. California was awash in black Porsches.
Anyway, what would a cowboy want with a vineyard?

Her cellular phone rang just as she reached the porch. She plucked it from her shoulder-bag and heard her attorney's voice.

"Ms. Thorpe, forgive me, but I'm afraid I'm going to be delayed."

Alex sighed, opened the screen door and stepped into the slate-floored foyer.

"Delayed? For how long?"

"Actually, I'm not sure I'm going to be able to make it at all. I tried calling you—"

"Never mind. We'll just have to reschedule."

"Well, if you'd be interested in a suggestion…"

She smiled at his new caution. "Certainly."

"You might wish to go ahead and hear what Mr. Baron has to say."

She felt the blood drain to her toes. "Who?"

"Mr. Baron. Travis Baron. I didn't realize you two were already acquainted, Ms. Thorpe, but Mr. Baron tells me that you're old friends."

"Old friends," Alex said, in a strangled whisper.

"It was the only thing I could think of telling him," a low male voice said.

Alex jerked around. Travis stood in the entrance to the living room. He was wearing jeans and a T-shirt, and those boots. Those cowboy boots…

"Alex? You are old friends, aren't you?"

She looked into the deep green eyes of the man she'd been dreaming about. They were not friends, and surely not old ones. They weren't even lovers. Not even she was naive enough to think that one long day spent in bed made a man and a woman into lovers.

"Alex?"

Alex licked her lips. "Yes," she said, into the phone, "yes, we're…we're old friends, Mr. Baron and I."

Travis smiled. She tried not to think of how his mouth tilted when he smiled, and how it had felt against her own.

"Good," her attorney said. "Fine. Just listen to what Mr. Baron has to say. Don't agree to anything, of course."

"Of course," Alex said, her eyes never leaving Travis, and she pressed the Disconnect button. "Mr. Baron." Her voice was cool but her hand was trembling as she put the phone away, and she hoped he couldn't see it.

"Back to formalities, Princess?"

Alex flushed. "Perhaps you'd like to explain your presence."

"Explain what? I'm here to buy this place. Didn't your lawyers tell that to you?"

"You? Buy Peregrine? You might have fooled my attorneys, but you can't fool me. What are you really doing here?"

Travis fought back the desire to take Alex in his arms and kiss that haughty look from her face. He'd imagined this scene over and over. Sometimes, she'd flown into his arms the second she saw him; in another version, she'd launched herself across the room and tried to scratch out his eyes.

What he hadn't anticipated was that she'd look at him as if he were something beneath contempt, or that she'd be even more beautiful than he remembered. He felt the stir of his body, looked at the disdain in her expression, and knew that nothing had changed.

Realizing it made him angry. Angry at himself, angry at her. No, anger didn't quite cut it. Fury was a better word, but he'd be damned if he was going to let her know it.

"What do you mean, what am I doing here?" he said calmly. He leaned back against the wall and tucked his hands into the back pockets of his jeans. "I'm here to talk about buying a vineyard."

"And the moon is made of green cheese."

"Is it?" he said pleasantly. "I've always wondered."

Alex drew herself up. "Look, I don't know how you managed to fool my attorneys into thinking you were really interested in—"

"I am," he said.

Her smile was icy. "You're interested in buying a vineyard?"

"Well, no. Not exactly."

"But you thought nothing of lying to my people, of dragging me up here on a fool's errand—"

"I represent Baron Enterprises."

"Baron Enter…"

She blinked, and a flush rose in her cheeks. Damn, it was good to see her take the first step toward a plate filled with crow.

"That's right," Travis said coolly. He took out his wallet, extracted a business card and held it out. "I'm a partner in the firm of Sullivan, Cohen and Vittali. I represent my father, Jonas Baron, who wants to buy your vineyard."

She took the card. Her eyes flashed from its heavy engraving to him, and Travis felt a curl of satisfaction in his belly as that disdainful look was replaced by confusion.

"You're an attorney?"

"Yes. I specialize in corporate law." He smiled, leaned away from the wall and folded his arms over his chest. "Perhaps you recognize the name of my firm."

She did. It was a law firm with a reputation and influence the equal of the one that represented her.

"And—and you say your father…"

"Is interested in buying this vineyard." Travis strolled past her, to the open door, and stepped onto the porch. "Maybe I should say he *was* interested."

Alex swung around and looked at him. "What is that supposed to mean?"

"Only that from what I've seen so far, I'm not inclined to recommend he continue with the purchase."

Those were the last words she'd expected to hear, and she couldn't keep her surprise from showing.

"Why not?"

"Do you know anything about viniculture?"

Her eyes narrowed. "No."

"Well, it's too complicated to explain, but—"

"Don't patronize me," she snapped.

Travis's brows rose. The Princess might not know anything about wine-making. From what he'd been able to learn during the past week, he doubted she knew much about half of what she'd inherited. Still, the tilt of her chin, coupled with that arrogant tone, said she was damned if she wasn't determined to learn.

Or maybe the only thing she wanted was to give him a hard time. Either way, it didn't matter. Peregrine Vineyards was a handsome place. It had charm. It even had possibilities. But it sure as hell wasn't worth the price her attorney had quoted.

"Well? I'm waiting to hear why my vineyard doesn't meet your high standards, Mr. Baron."

On the other hand, it was worth almost anything to see her eyes flash that way. Travis tried to look thoughtful as he glanced at his watch.

"I could fill you in on some of my thoughts over an early supper."

"I didn't come here for supper!"

"What did you come here for, then?" He looked up, his gaze noncommittal. "Do you want to sell this vineyard or don't you?"

"You just said there isn't going to be any sale."

Travis couldn't help it; he grinned. "I take it you've never been to Morocco."

Alex looked at him as if he'd lost his mind. "What does Morocco have to do with this?"

"And I'll bet you've never been to a flea market, either."

"What on earth are you talking about?" she demanded irritably.

"Whether you've buying a rug in the Casbah, Princess, or a painting of Elvis on velvet at the Swap Meet—"

"A painting on velvet?"

"Yeah. Don't you have one of those, in that castle you call home?"

Alex's eyes met Travis's. He was laughing. She told herself there was nothing funny happening here but a laugh burst from her throat, anyway.

"No. No, I can't say that I have."

"I can see where your education in the arts has been sadly neglected. The thing is, the first rule of selling is that you have to convince the buyer that he absolutely, positively must have the thing you want to sell him."

Alex smiled. "Ah. Then, I have something you want?"

Travis's smile tilted. "Yeah," he said softly, "you definitely do."

"I meant Peregrine," she said quickly.

"Of course." His tone was bland. "So did I. Well, then. Dinner, Ms. Thorpe?"

She hesitated. Her heart was dancing; she felt as if all the air were being drawn out of the room. But she'd come here to make a deal, and what kind of businesswoman would shy away from something so simple as dinner?

"Certainly," she said, and tried not to think too hard about the tingle that shot through her as Travis took her elbow and led her from the farmhouse.

He drove the Porsche too fast.

She'd driven almost this fast only once, a long time ago. It was when she'd owned a little convertible, a present for her eighteenth birthday from her father. His secretary had phoned, asking what she wanted as a gift, and Alex had taken a deep breath and said she'd love a red Miata. The secretary—a new one, which probably explained how it had happened, said fine. And, on the day she turned eighteen, the car was in the driveway with a Happy Birthday card from her from her father.

Within the first month of driving it, she'd gotten a speeding ticket. As soon as her father found out, the red convertible disappeared and the first in a long line of big, safe Mercedes had taken its place.

Even that one time she'd pushed the convertible to its limits, she'd never driven as fast as Travis was driving now.

She had no idea what road they were on. It was narrow and curving, completely unlike the straight, boring highway she'd taken from the airport in San Francisco. Travis took the turns easily, tucking the Porsche into the curves so that it held the road as if it was nailed to it. And on the occasional straight stretches, she saw the speedometer needle skyrocket.

He glanced over, once, and caught her peering at the dash.

"Is this too fast for you?" he said, and she shook her head and said no, it was fine, when what she wanted to say was that it was wonderful, and was it at all possible he'd pull over and switch places with her?

She sat back and folded her hands in her lap.

What was the matter with her, that she got such crazy ideas when she was around this man? Going to dinner with him, when every instinct screamed it was a mistake. Yearning to get behind the wheel of his car and stand on the gas pedal until the car flew for her as it was flying for him. Doing what she'd done two weeks ago, letting him make love to her, making love to him when she didn't know him at all, didn't even like him.

Well, maybe she did like him, just a little. He was arrogant, yes. And too darned sure of himself. But he was all-fire gorgeous. And sexy. He had a nice sense of humor. And she already knew what a fantastic lover he was.

Not that she'd ever go to bed with him again. Her one and only one-night stand was history. Besides, she had about as much in common with Travis Baron as a sparrow had with a cat.

Alex's pulse quickened.

It was just that cats, especially the big ones, were so beautiful, so lithe, so powerful and so incredibly exciting.

She sat back. Stop that, she told herself, but she knew she was blushing.

*   *   *

What could Alex be thinking, to put that sudden crimson stain on her beautiful cheekbones?

Travis sneaked a quick look at her again, then looked back at the road.

The more he saw of her, the deeper an enigma she became. Her on-and-off sexuality had almost driven him crazy, but there was more than that about her that he just couldn't figure out. From what he'd been able to gather, neither could her lawyers.

He'd been trying to figure a way to wangle a meeting with Alex, but things had fallen into place with surprising ease.

"Ms. Thorpe wishes to meet with you, Mr. Baron," one of her attorneys had said.

"Does she know who I am?" Travis had asked, with quickened interest.

"Oh, no. She never even thought to ask your name. It's probably her divorce that makes her think she wants to take some small role in her business affairs."

"How long ago was the divorce?"

"Two years." The attorney had sighed. "But I'm sure the stress lingers."

"Was she in love with her husband?"

If the attorney thought the question rather personal, he was too well-trained to show it.

"Of course," he'd replied.

Travis eased the car down to the speed limit as the road began its descent, and glanced at Alex again. Was that why she'd come on to him the way she had? Because she was heartbroken over the loss of her husband? It was possible; he could imagine a woman, in the depths of despair, trying to erase the memories of another man by going to bed with a stranger.

His jaw tightened.

Hell, he didn't want to think he'd been a second-best substitute for some guy who'd been stupid enough to lose this woman.

"Your husband," he said abruptly.

Alex swung her head toward him. "My ex-husband."

"Yeah." Travis's hands tightened on the wheel. "Who divorced who?"

"I beg your pardon?"

"Did you leave him, or was it the opposite way around?"

Alex touched the tip of her tongue to her lips. "I don't see what that has to do with Peregrine Vineyards."

Travis wrenched the wheel, hard, to the right. The brakes protested as he swung onto the narrow gravel shoulder and let the car idle.

"I was married," he said harshly. "I found my wife in bed with another man and realized I'd known for a long time, that I really didn't love her and maybe I never had." His green gaze caught hers and held it. "I wasn't trying to get rid of ghosts when I made love to you."

Alex's eyes widened. "I never said—"

"Were you?"

She swallowed dryly. "Was I—was I thinking about Carl when we—when you and I—"

"When you cried out, in my arms," Travis said, his eyes never leaving hers. "Were you thinking of him, wishing he was in your bed instead of me?"

She stared at him. It was a question he had no right to ask, one she had every right to refuse to answer. At the very least, she could lie, tell him yes, she'd been thinking about her ex when she'd been with him...

"Alex?"

Travis wasn't touching her but she could almost feel the strength of his hands on her. She wanted to feel them, to feel him against her.

She thought, for a second, she'd spoken the words aloud because he muttered a low curse, undid his seat belt, drew her to him in a rough embrace and kissed her. It was a long, deep kiss that made her heart race. When it ended, she was shaken.

"I need to know," he said, cupping her face and looking deep into her eyes. "Was it me, in your bed, or was it him?"

The lies, and the protection they offered, disappeared like a magician's rabbit.

"It was you," she whispered. "From the second you first kissed me, it was you."

They sat staring at each other, Travis's body hardening with need, Alex's softening with it. Then he drew away from her and reached for the gearshift.

"And a damn good thing it was," he said roughly, and the car fishtailed as he accelerated onto the road.

He took her to a little restaurant in a handsome inn perched by the seaside, and settled her at a table for two in an outdoor garden. The sun was just starting to droop against the cloudless sky.

Alex couldn't think straight. She let Travis order for the both of them and after their salads arrived, she bent her head and tried to concentrate on hers but the silence screamed at her and, at last, she looked up.

"It's beautiful here," she said.

"Why?" Travis said.

She tried to smile. "Why is it beautiful?"

"Why did you tell me to leave that night?" A muscle knotted in his jaw. "I wanted to make love to you again, Princess. And everything about you told me it was what you wanted, too."

Alex colored. "Please. I don't want to—"

"I can't get it out of my head. The way it was between us. The feel of you. The taste…"

Her fork clattered to the tabletop. "Travis," she whispered, "don't. What happened, what I did, was wrong. It embarrasses me to think about it, much less to discuss it."

He reached for her hand and caught it in his. "Listen to me, Princess. I'm not a kid. I've been with a lot of women. And I'm telling you, something incredible happened between us. How in hell can you say it was wrong?"

"Because…" She tugged her hand free of his. "Because

it was. I've never—I know you won't believe this, but I've never done anything like that before.''

His mouth curved in a smile. "You mean, you never paid twenty thousand dollars for a date before?"

"Go ahead," she said fiercely. "Laugh. But it isn't funny. I never picked up a man in my entire life. And I certainly never went to bed with a stranger I'd just..." She flung back her chair and shot to her feet. "I can't talk about this," she said, and ran from the restaurant.

Travis pulled some bills from his wallet, stuck them under the pepper mill and went after her. She was halfway down the deserted beach, walking with her arms wrapped around herself, her face turned to the sea, when he caught up to her.

"All right," she said, before he could speak. "Okay, Travis. You want to know what happened that night?" She swung towards him, her face pale. "I'll tell you."

"Alex." He wanted to take her in his arms but the look in her eyes warned him not to. "Princess, all you have to tell me was that I wasn't a guy standing in for somebody else."

Alex gave a bitter laugh. "I found my husband in bed with the woman I'd thought was my best friend. That was more than two years ago, and I remember thinking, almost calmly, that now, at least, I had a legitimate reason for ending a marriage I hated. No, Travis. you weren't standing in for a man I'd loved and lost. I—I bid on you that night to—to prove something to myself."

That look of ferocity was still in her eyes but there was a vulnerability to her mouth that made him ignore all the little warning lights going off in his head. He reached out and gently pushed a strand of her hair behind her ear, and then he let his hands drift to her shoulders. He held her gently, afraid that if he held her the way he wanted to, she'd run off again.

"What?" he said softly. "That you were beautiful?

Desirable? That any man who'd choose another woman over you ought to have his head examined?''

She rewarded him with a faint smile but when he tried to draw her closer, she pulled away.

"My husband said I was frigid. His exact words for me were that I was a frigid little rich bitch.''

Travis's eyes narrowed. "And you believed him?''

"I didn't really care. It meant—it meant he left me alone. Sex had been—it had been unsatisfying.''

"Unsatisfying,'' Travis repeated softly, in a way that made her shudder.

"Travis.'' She put her hand on his arm. The muscles were like stone under her fingers. "Travis, I'm only telling you this because—because I've finally admitted the truth to myself, that you deserve an explanation.''

He caught her hand in his, held it so tightly that she caught her breath.

"Go on,'' he said harshly. "Tell me more about this husband of yours.''

"There isn't much more to tell. As I said, I found him with another woman. And I divorced him.''

"And?''

"And,'' Alex said quietly, "that Friday afternoon, before the auction, I was in the ladies' room at a restaurant and I overheard two women talking about me. They said—they said they could tell just from looking at me that everything Carl's wife—''

"Your ex's wife?''

She nodded. "They said everything she'd been telling them was true, that I was a spoiled little rich girl with too much money and not enough libido. And I could tell, from how they said it, that all the people who were supposed to be my friends were probably scurrying around behind my back, discussing my sex life, too.''

Travis's hand fell from hers. "Go on.''

"I went shopping. I bought that dress. The underwear.

The shoes." She closed her eyes against the memory. "Then I burst into that stupid auction and I saw you."

"And you bought me."

Alex winced. "I—I made that bid, yes," she said, her voice as brittle as paper.

"I see."

The coldness of the words sliced through her self-pity. Alex looked up and saw the darkness in Travis's eyes.

"I was right, then," he said. "Your husband was in that bed with us."

"No! Oh, no."

"Maybe not because you were mourning his loss, but he was there, just the same." His mouth twisted. "So he could see you perform, and know what he was missing."

Alex hissed through her teeth and took a step back.

"It's amazing," she said, her voice trembling, "how I seem to specialize in making myself look stupid in front of you. Is that all you can think of? Your own pathetic ego? Yes, I bid on you out of anger. And yes, maybe it was anger that drove me to—to respond to you, in that doorway." She lifted her chin in defiance. "But what happened when you came to my home had nothing to do with anger, or with Carl, or with those witches in the ladies' room at L'Orangerie." Angry tears glittered in her eyes. "And I don't know why I thought I owed this explanation to you, Mr. Baron, because, frankly, I hate—"

Travis's mouth came down on hers.

CHAPTER NINE

THE thunder of the surf against the shore seemed no louder than the thundering beat of Alex's heart.

Travis's kiss was everything she had remembered, and more. She felt as if he were demanding the surrender of her soul as well as her body, but that wasn't true. How could it be, when the only thing between them was desire?

Oh, but such desire.

Travis's hands were in her hair, tipping her face up to his, holding her a willing prisoner as his mouth ravaged hers. It was a hard, possessive embrace, almost savage in its urgency. You belong to me, it said, to me and to no other man.

She knew it was an illusion. She didn't belong to him. She didn't want to; she had belonged to her father, then to her husband.

But Carl had never made her feel like this.

Travis whispered her name, sucked her bottom lip into his mouth. She moaned and wound her arms around his neck, lifted herself to him and shuddered with excitement when she felt the rigidity of his arousal hard against her belly.

His hands were under her blouse. She trembled as his callused fingertips rode her hot skin.

"Travis," she said, her voice broken and husky, "Travis..."

"My Princess," he said, and his hands swept up the soft underside of her breasts and cupped them.

Need roiled through her blood but she fought it back. *Don't*, she told herself, *don't do this, Alexandra. Remember how you felt the last time, the terrible feeling of emptiness, the self-loathing...*

Remember the feel of him within you, the blinding pleasure of his body in yours. Remember that moment when you tumbled off the edge of the earth and exploded in the heavens but most of all, most of all, remember how it felt afterward, lying in his arms, so at peace, so replete with happiness...

"Give yourself up to me," Travis whispered, against her throat. "Come with me, Alex, come with me and let me show you how it can be."

A hot, sweet wave of desire swept over her. Lost to it, she reached for him but his hand clamped down on hers.

"No," he said thickly. "Let me do this. Let me do it all."

She whimpered as he drew back, and the knowledge that she didn't want him to leave her was almost more than he could endure. He imagined having her now, pulling her down to the sandy beach in the darkness, rolling her under him, entering her on one long, hard thrust and riding her until she shattered in his arms.

It was how he'd taken her before, swiftly and with an elemental hunger. But it was not how he wanted to take her now, especially when the words she'd spoken with such terrible dispassion still echoed in his head.

Sex had been unsatisfying.

That was what she'd said, this woman who burned in his arms. Sex, with her husband, had been unsatisfying. He knew what it meant, that she had been a dutiful wife, that the son of a bitch who'd taken her to his bed had given nothing and taken everything.

Tonight, he would change that forever...but not if he gave in to the animal instincts that drove him. It took all his strength to stop her from touching him but even more than he wanted Alex, he wanted to give her this night.

"No," he said. "Not here."

"Of course." She stepped back. "I'm sorry, Travis. You're right. I should never have…"

"Dammit," he said roughly, and hauled her into his arms again. He kissed her, over and over, until she was clinging to him. "Don't ever apologize for wanting me. Don't you know how exciting that is, Princess? To know you feel the way I feel?" He took a deep breath, clasped her face gently in his hands and brushed his mouth over hers in a soft, lingering kiss. "I have a suite at the inn. It's where I planned on spending the night. Will you come there with me, and let me make love to you as if this were our first time?"

He waited for her answer, knowing that giving her time to think was a gamble. He was asking her to admit her need for him instead of being swept away by it, but he didn't want her to come to him blinded by passion.

Not tonight. Tonight, he wanted to seduce her. Awaken her. And to know, after this, the only man she would remember would be him.

"Alex." He ran his thumb over her parted lips. "I want to make love to you. Tell me it's what you want, too."

Her answer was in the soft surrender of her kiss.

His bedroom was high in the round turret of the handsome old inn.

The night's darkness held the room in close embrace, save for the ivory path laid across the bed by the moon.

Travis shut the door and locked it. The turn of the lock seemed to echo through the silent room.

Alex shivered.

There'd been no time for thinking, or for fear, when she'd gone to bed with him that other time. Desire had made her a creature of instinct, not of logic.

This was different. Travis had given her a choice and she'd made it. It was her decision that had brought her here, to his bed.

What would he expect from her, and what could she give him? If she failed him, she would fail herself…

"I can't do this," she said, and spun toward the door, straight into Travis's waiting arms. "Travis. Travis, please. I can't."

She was trembling. What was she afraid of? Of him? Of herself? Of the passion he had unleashed in her, that last time? She sighed, and he felt the warmth of the exhalation against his throat.

"What is it, Princess? Why are you afraid?"

She drew a shaky breath. "There was no time to think, before. It's why everything was... Travis. I'm not—I'm just not—"

"What?" he whispered, and kissed her, slowly, gently, his lips coaxing hers to soften and cling.

Alex gave a choked laugh and buried her face against his shoulder. "You'll laugh."

Travis gathered her closer. "Tell me."

"I'm not...experienced. I know that sounds silly, after the way I acted with you, but—"

"I don't believe you."

She shut her eyes in misery. "I didn't think you would. But what I told you is the truth. I've never—I've never been with any man except for my husband, and you."

"I believe that, with all my heart." He smiled and stroked his thumbs along her cheekbones. "But I don't believe you acted when we were together last time."

"Acted?" She drew back and looked up at him. "No. Oh, no. Everything I did and said was—"

"Real."

"Yes. But this isn't going to be the same. I can feel the difference already. I'm all the things I've always been when it comes to—to bed."

Travis gritted his teeth. Alex's husband really had been a bastard but he didn't want to think about that now. He wanted to think only of Alex.

"Yes," he said calmly, "you *are* all the things you've always been. You're beautiful." He feathered kisses over her face. "Desirable." He smiled. "And incredibly sexy, even without that red dress."

Alex shook her head. "That dress! I can't believe I bought it, or that I wore it. Carl used to say—"

"I don't give a damn what Carl used to say." Travis shut his eyes, told himself to take it easy. Pretending the wall was her ex's face and putting his fist through it was not going to make things better. "Listen to me, Princess. If you've changed your mind about making love with me, tell me so. But if your ex is lodged inside your head, I know exactly how to get rid of him."

Alex's smile trembled. "I don't think you can."

"Will you let me try?"

She looked up at him. "I'd like to. But—"

Travis took her into his arms. "Do you hear the music, Princess?"

She did. It was drifting in through the open windows, along with the soft, sighing breaths of the sea.

"Dance with me," he said, and he began moving to the slow, romantic tune.

She felt silly, at first, dancing in a darkened bedroom. Dancing was something you did in a ballroom, each of you with one arm outstretched, your hand on your partner's shoulder and his placed lightly in the small of your back. It was what Miss Mallory had taught her in Etiquette class, when she was a girl.

But Travis had broken those rules the first night they'd met, when he'd held her hard against him as he'd whirled her around and around the ballroom of the Hotel Paradise.

Now, he was breaking them again. Both his arms were around her, his hands low on her spine. And this was no dance that took a couple around the floor in light, graceful movements as Miss Mallory had taught. It was a dance a woman could only learn from a man who desired her.

"Relax," he whispered, "and feel the music."

What she felt was him. His heat. His breath. The tightly leashed power of his body, the steady beat of his heart.

Alex closed her eyes and put her head on Travis's shoulder. His arms tightened around her. One hand dropped lower, to spread across her bottom; the other slid slowly up her spine. He curled his fingers around her nape and toyed with her hair.

"I like your hair this way," he murmured.

"Tied back? It's the way I always..."

"I like it because it's kept me thinking, of how it would be to take it down." He drew back and looked down at her. "Shall I undo your hair, Alex?"

His voice was low, rough as raw silk. She felt a tightening in her breasts, and in the pit of her belly.

"Yes," she said, her eyes on his. "Yes, please. Undo—"

Her breath caught as he unclasped the barrette at the back of her neck. Her hair spilled over her shoulders, and over his hand. He lifted a handful of it, brought it to his lips.

"Beautiful," he said softly, and kissed her.

They swayed with the music. Mouth to mouth. Breast to breast. His thigh just between hers. Alex sighed. Travis kissed her hair, the shell of her ear.

"Look," he whispered.

She blinked, opened her eyes. They were in front of a floor-to-ceiling mirror, locked in each other's arms, bathed in the soft light of the moon.

"Do you see how beautiful you are?" Travis said.

Alex flushed. "Travis..."

He moved behind her, lifted her hair and let it sift like gold over his fingers. He bent his head and pressed his mouth to her neck, and then he began undoing the tiny buttons that ran down the back of her silk blouse. He opened them slowly, pausing to kiss each bit of newly exposed skin. At last, when they were all undone, he slid the blouse from her shoulders.

Her bra was made of unadorned white cotton. It was nothing like the stuff she'd worn the night they met but that didn't matter. There was something about her reticence, her trust, that made this bit of utilitarian cotton sexier than any concoction of black lace could ever be. Was that why his fingers shook as he undid the clasp?

He watched her face in the mirror as her breasts tumbled into his waiting palms.

If she looked at him like that again, he'd be finished. It was too much to ask of a man, that he hang onto his sanity while a beautiful woman stared at him as if he were showing her all the secrets of the universe. But he had to hang on, had to make this right, for her.

His hands cupped her breasts, his thumbs skimming over her nipples.

"Travis…"

Her voice was a tremulous whisper. She tried to turn toward him, away from what she saw in the glass, but he wouldn't let her.

"Not yet," he whispered.

He nuzzled her hair aside, so it fell over one bare shoulder. He bent his head and kissed her nape, nipped lightly at her throat. Alex had to bite her lip to keep from crying out. She was drowning in a river of sensation but she couldn't, she couldn't. If she let the river sweep her away, how would she know if she was doing all the things a woman should?

Travis was wrong. She couldn't get Carl out of her head this time. He was there, telling her that she was unresponsive, that she didn't know how to please a man and never would.

And she wanted to please Travis. To give him pleasure. To hear him groan as he spent himself inside her…

His thumbs rubbed across her nipples again, and the cry she'd tried so hard to suppress burst from her throat. Her head fell back against his shoulder.

"Travis," she whispered, and he cupped her breasts again, holding them, molding them, stroking the swollen peaks until, without thinking, she lifted her hands and placed them over his before she realized what she'd done and she snatched her hands away.

"Do that," Travis said thickly. "Put your hands over mine."

"No. I mean—not if you don't like... Not if you think it's—it's wrong..."

"Open your eyes, Princess. Look into the mirror."

She thought of that day two weeks before, when she'd looked into the mirror and seen what Travis's passion had done to her, of how horrified and humiliated she'd been.

"No," she said, "Travis, please. I don't—"

"Just look," he whispered.

And, slowly, she did.

The woman in the mirror wasn't her. It was a woman trembling on the brink of surrender. Her hair was tumbled around her naked shoulders. Her mouth was pink and swollen, her eyes were feverishly bright.

And the man who'd made her look like this stood just behind her, staring at her reflection with such naked hunger that it made her dizzy.

"Go on," he said softly, his eyes never leaving hers. "Cover my hands with yours."

Color swept into her face. "Carl said—he said it was wrong to do that. It would be like touching myself."

"Put your hands over mine, Alex."

Their eyes met. Slowly, she raised her hands and did as he'd asked. The sight electrified her. His skin, so dark and hers, so pale; his hands so large and powerful, hers so small and feminine...

"There's nothing you can't do with me, Princess." He bent his head, kissed her throat. "There are no rights and wrongs, not between us. Do you understand?"

"Yes," she whispered.

"There's only you, and me, and what pleases us both." Her hands fell away from his as he let go of her breasts. His fingers went to the fly front of her linen trousers. She felt the button give, heard the hiss of the zipper. Her trousers slipped down her legs and fell to her feet. "Tell me what

pleases you, Alex,'' Travis said, and cupped the damp silk
between her thighs.

Alex cried out, not only with need but with the shock of
realization. She'd thought Travis had been in her dreams for
the past two weeks. Now, she knew he'd been in them forever, this handsome, dangerous, tender stranger who'd come
into her carefully planned world and turned it upside down.
He was no longer a dream. He was flesh and bone and
blood, his eyes pools of darkness, his body hers to lean
against, his hands hers to watch as they touched her.

"Do you like this?" he whispered, and slipped his fingers
under the silk. "And this?"

She exploded against him, her body's most intimate tears
scalding his hand with her heat as she called out his name.

It almost undid him.

And it would almost have been enough. Just to see her
lovely face as she came, to know his strength was her support, to hear her say his name as if he was the only man
she'd ever want, ever need...

It was more than most men would ever know of heaven.

And yet, he wanted more.

He turned her in his arms, drew her against him, lifted
her off her feet so that her head was above his and he kissed
her, swallowing the last of her cries, knowing that he—and
only he—had brought her such pleasure.

Would ever bring her such pleasure.

Slowly, he lowered her the length of his body.

"Undress me," he said, against her mouth.

She tried, but her hands were shaking. And he couldn't
wait, not anymore. He undressed them both, scattering his
clothes and hers, tearing things, ripping them in his desperate haste to carry her to the bed, sink into her silken heat,
to cover her soft body with the hardness of his. Gently, he
manacled her wrists with his hands and lifted her arms
above her head as he sucked on her breasts, licked her
throat, buried himself in her slowly, slowly, slowly until, at
last, she pleaded for release.

He let go of her hands and she wrapped her arms around him, wrapped her legs around him, took him so deeply inside her that he couldn't think. And, when he knew she was on the brink, he said, voice hoarse with passion, "Look at me, Alex. And say my name."

Her lashes lifted. Tears glittered like starlight in her eyes.

"Travis," she whispered. "Travis. Travis. Trav—"

He groaned, drove deep, and the world shattered for them both.

Travis awakened slowly, blinked his eyes against the sunshine and inhaled the sweet fragrance of the incredible woman who'd spent the night in his arms.

A smile spread across his mouth as he sent up a quick thank-you to whatever gods might be in the vicinity for letting him wake up and find that the night—the long, wonderful night—had not been a dream.

Carefully, moving so as not to disturb her, he rose on his elbow and gazed down at Alex's beautiful profile. She lay with her head pillowed on his arm and her backside snugged into the cradle of his hips.

Very snug, he thought, as the warmth of that curving bottom sent an early-morning wake-up call zinging through his blood.

But he wouldn't wake her. She needed her rest, after the night they'd spent. Besides, he wanted to watch her. Just watch her, as she slept.

Her hair streamed over her shoulder, a cascade of golden silk. Her lashes lay thickly on her cheeks. Her lips were slightly parted. One hand was tucked beneath her pillow; the other lay on top of it. It was a lovely hand, he thought, with long fingers and blunt-trimmed, unvarnished nails. Last night, he'd sucked those fingers into his mouth, one by one. Such a simple thing, but there'd been nothing simple in the way his body had tightened as he'd watched Alex's pupils grow black with each stroke of his tongue.

Hell.

Travis stifled a groan and drew back enough to put a discreet inch between Alex and himself. He'd made love to her endless times through the night but he wanted her again, right now, with a hunger so intense that he might as well have spent the past hours in a monastery.

He wouldn't touch her, though. Not yet. She was so soundly asleep.

But he could look.

Slowly, carefully, inch by tantalizing inch, he drew down the blanket that covered them.

How beautiful his Princess was.

The soft curve of her shoulder. The roundness of her arm. The fullness of her breasts and the curve of her hip...

The sweet, honeyed taste of her, against his seeking mouth.

His seeking mouth.

Travis rolled closer and kissed her throat. He kissed her shoulder, nuzzled her underarm. He stroked his hand gently along her until she sighed, rolled onto her back...

And awakened.

He watched her, knew the exact second she remembered where she was and what had happened. Would she regret it? Would she turn to ice, as she had the last time she'd awakened in his arms?

He waited, poised above her, for the first time in his life anticipating, and dreading, a woman's rejection.

If she tried to toss him out this time, he'd go without a word. Hell, no. He wouldn't do that. If she tried to toss him out, he'd pin her to the bed, kiss her until she admitted the truth, that she wanted him now, that she'd wanted him then...

A radiant smile curved Alex's lips.

"Good morning," she said, and held up her arms.

Travis went into them like a man returning home.

They drove back to the vineyard, this time walking through the endless rows of grapes with their arms around each other.

"I love it here," Alex said softly.

Travis looked down at the bright head nestled against his shoulder and smiled. "Then why are you selling it?"

She sighed and shrugged her shoulders. "Peregrine loses money, year after year."

"Well, of course it does."

Alex laughed, drew away from Travis's encircling arm and plucked a leaf from a vine.

"I know this may astound you, Mr. Baron, but a property is supposed to make money."

"This isn't a property, Ms. Thorpe. It's a philosophy."

"A philosophy," Alex deadpanned, stepping out in front of him. "Well, that explains it. I mean, all this time, my lawyers and accountants have been thinking it's a winery."

Travis grinned, grabbed her by the waist and spun her around.

"Growing grapes, making wine—it's a mystical experience, Princess."

"Uh-huh."

"Go on, scoff. I'm telling you the truth."

"So, in other words, if I light some incense, sacrifice a couple of chickens, maybe dance around a tree, naked, on a moonlit night..."

"I like the dancing naked part." Travis put his hand under her chin, tilted her mouth to his and kissed her tenderly. "But no, I didn't mean that kind of mystical experience. See, you have to love the whole wine-making gestalt."

"The gestalt," Alex said solemnly. "I don't know... is that anything like *goulash?* Because I have to tell you, Travis, I really don't like—"

She squealed as he dragged her into his arms and kissed her.

"Wine-making," he growled, "is best done by those who are willing to break their backs in the fields and empty their bank accounts just so they can someday point to a bottle of twenty-dollar vino and proudly say, 'There it is—and it only cost me fifty bucks to produce.'" He smiled. "In other words, you have to be nuts to go into this business."

Alex smiled into Travis's eyes, rose toward him and placed her hands on either side of his face.

"Nuts, like you?"

He caught her hand, brought it to his lips and kissed the palm.

"I've thought about it," he admitted.

"But?"

"But, I have a law practice, and a life four hundred miles south of wine country. Plus, establishing a winery with a vintage good enough to make it profitable takes years." He linked his fingers through hers and they started walking. "Like the grapes, you have to settle in, put down roots, commit yourself to making it all work..."

"Sounds a lot like marriage," Alex said lightly.

A muscle knotted in Travis's jaw. "Yeah. Yeah, I suppose it does." His hand tightened on hers. "And I've already gone that route, Princess. Settling down, marriage... It didn't work. Heck, it doesn't seem to work very well for any of the Baron clan."

"I'm not sure it works for anybody." Alex raised her eyes to his. "I'm not looking for marriage," she said bluntly, "if that's what you're asking. My mother was unhappy with my father, right up until the day she died. And my marriage...well, you already know about that." She took a deep breath. "I was an obedient daughter, and belonged to my father. Then I was a dutiful wife, and belonged to my husband. Now, I don't want to belong to anybody but myself."

Travis nodded, reached out and tucked a flyaway strand of hair behind her ear.

"That sounds perfect, Princess. And I'm glad we got it all out of the way, right upfront."

They smiled at each other and then Travis cleared his

throat. "So," he said briskly, "did I happen to mention I flew my own plane here, from L.A.?"

"No," Alex said, just as briskly, "no, you didn't. You mean, that Porsche isn't yours?"

He grinned. "You'd be amazed how hospitable a dealer can be when he knows a guy's a sucker for every new Porsche that comes blowing into town. What do you say, Princess? Will you trust yourself to me for the flight home?"

She smiled. "Absolutely."

Travis smiled, too. How lucky could a man get? He'd found a beautiful, wonderful woman, one who pleased him more than any other he'd ever known. And she'd made it clear that she didn't want to smell orange blossoms, or hear wedding bells...

"Come here," he said gruffly.

He gathered her into his arms and kissed her...and tried not to let it trouble him that she'd basically just told him she was more willing to trust him with her life than with her heart.

CHAPTER TEN

TRAVIS had been flying his own plane since he was a kid.

So had all the Barons. Espada sprawled over so many thousands of acres that there were times it made more sense to cross it by plane than by horse or Jeep.

He loved to fly, loved the freedom he found in the air. But he'd never enjoyed it as much as he did on the trip back to Los Angeles.

And it was all because of Alex.

He could tell that she was a little nervous, when she first climbed into the Comanche.

"It's smaller than I'd expected," she said, flashing him a quick smile as she secured her seat belt.

Travis looked around as if he'd never seen his plane before. Compared to the Ultra-Light he and the rest of the Los Lobos gang had built the summer he was fifteen, the four-passenger Comanche was downright enormous. On the other hand, he figured it might seem a bit cramped if a person had only flown in the first-class compartment of a jumbo jet.

"It's not too late to change your mind, Princess," he said.

Alex shook her head. "Oh, no!" She looked at him, and he marveled at the rosy flush of pleasure in her cheeks. "I want to try everything, Travis, all the things people said were inappropriate." She laughed. "Even the things *I* said were inappropriate."

He grinned. "Like what?"

"Oh, I don't know. Everything. Eating a hot dog bought from a pushcart."

"Ah. Definitely a gourmet experience, not to be missed."

"Go on, laugh. But it's something I always wanted to do."

"I am not laughing, Princess." Travis grinned. "Why would a guy laugh, when he finds out his woman would rather have him spring for a two-buck hot dog than a two-hundred-dollar meal at the latest bistro?"

"Is that what I am?" Alex said, her color deepening. "Your—your woman?"

"Yes." His smile tilted. "I know what you said—what we both said—about not getting tied down, about not wanting commitment, but while you're with me—"

"For as long as it lasts, you mean."

"That's right. For as long as it lasts, you're mine."

The angle of his jaw dared her to argue. What would he do if she did? If she said, I'll sleep with as many men as I want...

Except, it would be a lie. How could she want any man, after Travis? How could she ever want...

"Alex? If you don't like the ground rules, tell me. Because I don't share." His voice roughened as their eyes met. "You see only me. You sleep only with me."

"Are the rules the same for you?"

His mouth twisted. "Yes."

She nodded. "All right."

"Okay, then. That's settled." A minute went by, and then Travis cleared his throat. "So, what else is on this Wish List of yours, Princess?"

She smiled. "Oh, lots of other dumb things."

"For instance?"

"Well...driving a car like your Porsche."

"Aha. The lady has a hankerin' to put the pedal to the metal, hmm?"

"I had a little convertible once," she said dreamily. "A red one..."

"And?"

Alex gave herself a brisk shake. "This is silly. I'm a grown woman, Travis. These are childhood wishes—"

He reached across the seat and took her hand. "My very first car was a red convertible."

She looked at him. "Really?"

"Uh-huh. It was a Mustang, so old it was damn near an antique." He flashed her a quick smile. "Took me a whole year of savin' up to buy it, too. What I got paid for workin' the barns. Rodeo money—"

"Rodeo...?" Alex laughed. "I was right! You *are* a cow-boy."

"I rode bulls." He squeezed her hand, took his away and laid it back on the Comanche's yoke. "I had some crazy dream of becoming champion."

"Whoops," she said, "there's got to be a lawyer joke here somewhere. Like, it takes a lawyer to turn a bull into a steer..."

"Very funny," Travis said wryly. "What happened was, my second time out, I got two ribs busted and my nose broke. So I decided maybe there was a better way of making a dollar than getting my neck broke."

Alex clasped her hands in her lap. "Ah."

"Ah, what?"

"That explains the nose. I wondered how that had happened."

"Uh-huh." Travis touched his finger to the bump. "I was gonna have it fixed but Catie said—"

"Catie?"

"My stepsister. She said it would drive the girls wild." He chuckled. "So I let it alone."

Alex smiled. "Well, I'm glad you listened to Catie. She was right."

"Was she, now?"

"Stop fishing for compliments, Mr. Baron."

Travis laughed, reached for Alex's hand and brought it to his lips. "Okay, darlin'. Now you know I was once crazy enough to think I could be a bull rider. And that I had me a red Mustang."

"I love it when you lapse back into that drawl of yours."

"Me? Drawl? Why, darlin', whatever do y'all mean by that?" He smiled. "You going to tell me what else is on that list of yours, or do I have to guess?"

Alex sighed. "Honestly, it's all so silly... Okay. I always wanted to drive a fast car. And ride a roller coaster. Oh, and walk in the rain."

"You've never walked in the rain?"

"Not barefoot. Not without an umbrella. Not with my face turned up to the drops." She gave a little laugh. "I must sound like an idiot."

"You sound like a woman who's fallen into exactly the right hands, Ms. Thorpe," Travis said solemnly. "Here, right beside you, is a man who hates shoes—"

"That's because he prefers boots."

"Well, yeah." He chuckled. "But not on the beach, where I live."

"You live on the beach?"

"Uh-huh. I have a house at Malibu."

"Oh, that must be wonderful. The sea, the sand, the sky..."

"Now you're going to tell me you've never been to the beach," Travis said, with a little smile.

"Of course I've been to the beach. San Tropez. Martinique..."

"What about right here, in southern California?"

"The truth?"

"Uh-huh."

She laughed. "Never."

"Never? As in, not even once?"

"No. Carl and my father both thought too many liberal Hollywood-types owned houses on those beaches."

Travis shook his head. "What a deprived childhood you had, Ms. Thorpe! No wading in the water. No walking in the rain. No roller coasters or chili dogs..."

"Chili dogs?"

"Trust me on this, darlin'. A naked hot dog's nothin', compared to a chili..." Travis paused and pressed a button on the yoke. "Piper five-eight foxtrot." His voice was suddenly brisk, his tone all business. "Roger. Traffic left to right, across my heading."

Alex sat back, watching with fascination as Travis scanned the sky around them. He had so many faces—it amazed her, how readily she'd written him off that first night, that first weekend. Had she been afraid of letting herself see the real man? No. That was silly. Why would she have done that? The real man was the one she'd been searching for, when she'd gone into the auction on Friday night.

She'd wanted someone to teach her what sex was really like, and she'd found him. She'd wanted a lover women dream about—a lover she'd dreamed about, and she'd found that, too. Travis had awakened her to passion. She'd become a different woman, in his strong arms. And, when their affair ended, she'd walk away, head high.

She'd gone into this with her eyes open, not wanting a fairy-tale ending but her own identity. Her independence. She had a lot of years to make up for. The last thing she wanted was a man who'd demand things of her—aside from the pleasure she brought him in bed.

And she had brought him that pleasure. The things he'd whispered to her, the ways he'd touched her...oh yes, she'd made him happy, in bed.

But he wouldn't ask for more than that. Well, good. That was how she wanted it. It was exactly how she wanted it. She wanted a lover, in this new existence of hers, not a man interested in forever after.

She wanted Travis, just as he was.

Of course she did, Alex thought, and turned her face blindly to the window as the Comanche soared through the sky.

"I didn't mean we had to do it all tonight," Alex said, as she stared up at the huge steel structure that rose in stomach-bending loops, high above the Magic Mountain Amusement Park.

Travis clasped her hand in his. "We aren't," he said lazily. "So far, all we've done is have hot dogs—"

"Chili dogs," Alex said, and smiled. "Fantastic!"

"See what I mean, darlin'? You have to trust me. I said you'd love 'em, and you did." He jerked his head toward the 'coaster. "And you're gonna love that, too. Unless, of course, you've changed your mind."

"Just listen to you, Cowboy." Alex laughed. "You're trying to sweet-talk me into getting on that thing."

"I am, for a fact." Travis put his hand under her chin and tipped her face to his. "I won't let anything happen to you, Princess." He bent to her and brushed his mouth over hers. "I'll hold on to you, tight, all the way down."

She smiled into his eyes. "You promise?"

"Cross my heart." He drew her closer and kissed her, long and sweet. "I'll always take care of you, Alex," he said softly. "Always."

No, she thought, no, he wouldn't.

Her vision blurred again, the same as it had when they'd left the airport. But she managed to smile and kiss him back.

"In that case, Mr. Baron," she said lightly, "lead on."

But, once on the roller coaster, Alex screamed.

She shrieked.

She clung to Travis and swore she was going to die.

And, when the ride ended, she dragged him to the end of the queue and made him take her up again.

Travis figured she'd have begged for a third ride, if he hadn't diverted her attention by asking her if she'd ever tasted cotton candy.

"What's cotton candy?" she asked, wide-eyed.

He bought her a giant-size cone that had been dipped in what might have been endless yards of pink spun sugar. She tasted it cautiously, testing it with the tip of a tongue as pink as the candy. Travis felt his body clench as he watched her. A need so fierce it frightened him swept through his blood.

He wanted to gather her into his arms, carry her away from the noise and the people, take her to some quiet place where only the moon and the stars would look down on them as they made love.

"Oh," Alex said, "Travis, this is wonderful!"

He looked at her, at her smiling face and her sugar-studded lips.

"Wonderful," he said, in soft agreement, and he bent to her and touched his mouth to hers, drinking in the sweetness of the sugar and the sweetness that was uniquely Alex. "Wonderful," he whispered, and he drew her into the shadows and into his embrace.

Her arms went up and encircled his neck.

"Travis," she said, her voice trembling.

"Yes, Princess," he murmured, "yes, I know."

He didn't know. He couldn't. She didn't know, herself, couldn't imagine why her heart was racing. Why she suddenly wished they were alone, under the star-filled sky. So he could make love to her, yes, but for more than that. Oh, for so much more...

Travis cupped her face in his hands. He kissed her, gently at first, then with growing passion.

The cotton candy cone drooped from her fingers.

"Princess," he whispered. "Come home with me."

"Yes." Her eyes were bright as they met his. "Oh, yes."

He drove quickly through the night, yearning to touch her but wanting, needing, the sweet pain of anticipation.

He wanted her now, so badly that the thought of it nearly made him dizzy, the need for her curling through his blood like an aphrodisiac. And he could tell, by the way she'd trembled when he'd kissed her, that she wanted him the same way.

But he knew, too, that the first frenzy of their lovemaking wouldn't be enough. He'd want her again, slowly once he'd regained his sanity, taking all the time he needed to lose himself in her kisses, to stroke the satin skin between her thighs, taste the honeyed sweetness of her breasts.

No, he thought, as he urged the Porsche along the dark Coast Highway, no, he didn't dare touch her now.

He turned into his driveway. The electronic gate opened at the touch of a button, then closed silently behind them. The gravel road had never seemed as long, nor the trees alongside so high.

The garage loomed ahead but he didn't bother with it. He stopped the car, opened the door, stepped out into the sea-scented night and then she was in his arms.

"Travis," she whispered, and the yearning in her voice, the softness of her sigh, almost undid him. All his romantic plans, the sweet seduction he'd intended, were swept away by need.

He kissed her, holding her head between his palms, threading his hands into her hair, angling his mouth over hers again and again while she clung to him, her fingers knotting into his shirt, her mouth open and wild beneath his.

He scooped her into his arms, carried her up the wooden steps that led to the deck, his mouth never leaving hers. He could hear the sea pounding against the sand, like the heavy pulse of his own blood.

He let her down slowly, her body soft against the hardness of his, and fumbled in his pocket for the keys.

"Wait," he said thickly, and made one last attempt to hold on to his sanity.

But Alex couldn't wait. Her body tingled with the tension that had built between them in the car, all through the endless, silent drive; she had never wanted anything, needed anything, as she needed to feel Travis's arms around her.

She murmured his name, slipped between him and the door, her arms tight around his neck, her mouth open and enticing on his.

"Now," she said, "Travis, please, now."

She touched him, her hand sliding down over his erection, cupping him. She heard the metallic tinkle of the keys as they fell to the deck, heard his groan and then his hands were hard on her shoulders as he backed her against the

door. He lifted her skirt and she felt her panties rip, felt his
hand as he undid his zipper, and then he was inside her,
deep inside her, and the stars began to spin in the heavens.

"Alex," he whispered, as he cupped her bottom and
lifted her to him. "Alex."

"Travis." Her voice trembled. She wanted to say more,
to tell him what she felt...

But he moved, moved again. A high, keening cry burst
from her throat, and she was lost.

She awakened, alone in Travis's wide bed, as dawn
touched the room with wisps of pink and gold. Above, the
blades of a ceiling fan turned lazily.

Alex sighed, snuggled deeper under the blanket. Her muscles ached a little, her mouth was swollen. The delicate scent
of their lovemaking clung to her skin.

It had been a long night, a night filled with abandon.

And she felt wonderful.

She sighed again, stretched her arms, rolled onto her belly
and rubbed her cheek against the coolness of the pillowcase.

A smile curled across her lips. The case, the sheets, were
silk. The bed was enormous. All in all, the room had been
a perfect setting for the hours she'd spent in Travis's arms...

Her smile faded.

It *was* the perfect setting. The room had been designed
for this, for the seductions of a bachelor.

How many other women had shared this bed? There had
to have been many. A man like Travis wouldn't live a
monk's existence. How many others had died and been re-
born in his embrace, only to mourn his loss?

The real question was, how long before it would be her
turn?

Alex closed her eyes.

No commitment. No forever after. Just pleasure, for as
long as it lasted. That was the bargain they'd made. The
terms were mutual. She had discovered herself. She could
be independent, she could be free, she could be a sensual,
sexual woman.

Surely, that was enough. Wasn't it?

She rolled onto her back and stared blindly at the turning ceiling fan. She had everything she'd dreamed of. And yet, suddenly, she felt empty, felt—

The door swung open.

"Good morning, Princess," Travis said, and Alex sat up, dragging the sheet to her chin, while her heart flew into her throat.

He stood in the doorway, holding a tray in his hands. He was naked except for his unzipped jeans, his dark hair was mussed, there was a sexy stubble on his jaw and he was more gorgeous, more incredibly masculine, than any man had the right to be.

It would be so easy to fall in love with him.

The thought took her breath away. No. She could never do that, fall in love with a man like Travis, who didn't believe in commitment or forever after, and certainly not in love...

"I made us some breakfast." He smiled as he crossed the room and set the tray down on the nightstand beside her. "Bacon, eggs, toast and a gallon of coffee."

Say something, she told herself furiously, and somehow she managed to tear her gaze from his face and look at the tray.

"It's—it's enough for an army," she said, and forced a smile to her lips.

"Yeah." His smile turned into a devilish grin. "But I figured you might be as hungry as I am this morning."

She looked at him. She needed time to think, and she couldn't do that here, in his bed.

"Travis—"

"Besides, we have to keep up our strength." He kissed her. "Driving lessons tend to take a lot out of a person," he murmured, his mouth against her throat.

Alex blinked and drew back. "Driving lessons?"

"Yeah." He took a strip of crisp bacon from the tray, bit

off a piece, then put it to her lips. "Well, not driving lessons, exactly. Open up, Princess, and take a bite."

She did. Bacon had never tasted so ambrosial.

"Porsche lessons," Travis said, watching her, smiling when her blue eyes widened. "Unless, of course, you've changed your mind about wanting to see what it's like to handle a fast car..."

Alex gave a wild whoop, tossed back the sheet and sprang from the bed.

"Oh, Travis! No, I haven't changed my mind. I'd love to drive your car. Do you really mean it? Do you...? Travis? What's the matter?"

He looked at her. She stood with the glass deck doors at her back, limned by the light of the new day, naked and rosy and gently marked with the signs of his possession.

"Travis?"

He wanted to tumble her back down onto the bed, and make love to her again. Wanted to slip deep inside her and hear her soft little cries as he took her over the edge of the precipice.

"Travis, what is it?"

But mostly—mostly, he wanted to hold her in his arms. Just hold her, and never, ever let her go. Not today. Not tomorrow. Not...

He rose to his feet.

"I just remembered." His voice was gruff. "We'll have to put the Porsche lessons off until another time. I, uh, I have an appointment this morning."

"Oh." Her smile tilted. "Well, sure. Tomorrow, maybe. Or the next day..."

"I'll call you," he said. "When I have the time. How does that sound?"

Like a polite goodbye. That was how it sounded. The bastard! Had she really just been warning herself not to fall in love with him? Only a masochist would fall for a man like Travis Baron.

And here she was, standing naked in the middle of his bedroom.

She wanted to fold her arms over her body but she didn't. Instead, she reached for his shirt, which he'd discarded so eagerly the night before.

"It sounds fine," she said politely. "Although, now that I think of it, I'm going to be busy the next few days." Her fingers trembled as she buttoned the shirt from her throat to her thighs. "Do call me, though. I'm sure we can get together again."

He nodded. "Good. I'm, uh, I'm glad you understand..."

"Oh, I understand, Travis. Completely."

He nodded again. She *didn't* understand; he could hear it in her voice but whose fault was that? Not his, surely. He'd made his position clear. Okay, so maybe he'd been carried away a few minutes ago, making all those plans for them. She should have stopped him. Hadn't she said she wanted the same freedom he wanted? But that was the way women were. They said what they figured a guy wanted to hear, even if it was nothing but a bucket full of lies.

"Travis?"

He looked up. "Yeah?"

"I'd like to get dressed."

But not in front of him. She didn't have to say the words for him to hear them.

"Sure. Uh, if you'd like to use the shower..."

"I'll shower at home, thank you."

He nodded again. It was all he seemed capable of doing. "Fine," he said briskly. "I'll just be a couple of minutes, and then I'll drive you."

He walked into the bathroom, shut the door and stepped into the shower stall. Then he turned the water on full, bowed his head, pressed his hands flat against the marble wall and let the water beat down on his shoulders.

He should never have brought Alex home last night. Whatever had he been thinking? And what was all this stuff he'd gotten himself into, with her ridiculous Wish List? So

she'd never done a lot of things. Big deal. He'd never done
a lot of things, either. Never flown a jet. Never ridden a
balloon across the Pacific. Never really fallen in love without holding a part of himself back...

"Hell," he whispered. "Oh, hell."

But he wasn't in love. He never would be. He'd thought
he was before, and learned the hard way never to tie himself
to one woman for too long.

Alex would just have to accept that.

Travis shut off the water, stepped from the shower and
flung open the bathroom door.

"Alex," he said, "Alex, look..."

The words caught in his throat. His bedroom was empty.
Alex was gone.

CHAPTER ELEVEN

GONE? Where could she have gone without a car?

Travis pulled on his jeans, ran into the hall and down the stairs.

"Alex?"

The silence of the early morning echoed her name.

The front door stood open. He stepped outside, called for her again. There was no answer, and no sign of her.

Travis mouthed an oath. Barefoot, barechested, he got into his car and turned the key. The engine started with a roar; gravel flew as he made a U-turn and stepped hard on the gas.

She couldn't have gotten very far.

He might have known she'd run. Hey, she *always* ran. She'd run that first night, run when he'd confronted her the next day. She'd wanted to run at Peregrine, too, but he'd been too quick for her.

The gate at the end of the driveway was open. He gunned the Porsche through it, then stood on the brakes, glared left, then right...

There she was, marching determinedly along the shoulder of the highway, heading south toward Los Angeles. This time of the day, the road was jammed with vehicles, zipping by in a dizzying stream.

Travis jumped from the car and stormed toward her.

"Alex!"

She heard him. He knew she did; he could tell because she picked up her pace, But she didn't turn, didn't acknowledge his presence any other way.

A van shot past, horn blaring.

"Alex, dammit!" Travis caught up to her, grabbed her

arm and spun her toward him. Her face was flushed, her eyes and mouth narrowed.

"Let go!"

"What in hell do you think you're doing?"

"What does it look like I'm doing? Let go of me, Cowboy!"

"Don't be a bloody little idiot! You can't walk back home."

"I can do whatever I want to do, Mr. Baron." Alex bared her teeth. "Get your hand off me!"

"You're behaving like a child."

"I am neither a child nor an idiot." Her eyes flashed. "Let go or so help me, Travis, I swear—"

"I don't like people running out on me, Princess." He moved closer, his fingers biting into her flesh. "You should have figured that."

"I did not run." Her chin lifted a notch. "I left. And I don't have any reason to give a flying fig what you like and don't like."

"Alex, dammit—"

The sound of tires crunching on gravel made them both turn. A police car had pulled up behind them.

"Now see what you've done," Travis muttered.

"What I've done?" Alex glared at him. "What *I've* done?"

A uniformed officer stepped from the car. His smile was pleasant but his walk was purposeful and cautious as he approached them.

"'Morning, folks. Is there a problem here?"

Travis took a breath. "No problem, Officer. The lady and I are just having a, uh, a discussion."

The cop nodded. Travis felt the weight of his gaze as it swept over him, taking in his bare chest and feet and his hand wrapped around Alex's wrist.

"Is that what this is, ma'am? A discussion?"

"No," Alex said coldly, "it is not. This man—this man…"

"Do you know him?"

"Yes. And he..." She hesitated. There was nothing she could say that wouldn't make her want to crawl into a corner and hide. Could she tell the officer that she and Travis had spent the night together? That she'd run away because she felt used and cheap? That he'd come after her because he felt insulted, or maybe simply because he'd had second thoughts and decided the sex was too good to give up?

"Ma'am?"

Alex swallowed dryly. "I know him. And we're—we're having a disagreement, not a discussion."

"A disagreement," the cop said, in wearied tones that probably meant he'd heard it all before. "Well, if it's all the same to you, lady, it'd be a good idea if you took your disagreement back where it started."

"We will," Travis said grimly, his hand tightening on Alex's. "We were just on our way back to my place. Weren't we, Alex?"

She looked at him and he knew she'd liked to have tried clawing out his eyes, if they'd been alone.

"Yes," she said through her teeth.

"And you're going with him willingly, ma'am?"

Alex sighed. "Yes, Officer."

The cop nodded, folded his arms and waited. Alex wrenched her hand free of Travis's. Head high, shoulders back, she marched back to the gate. Travis, feeling like an idiot, muttered something about having a nice day and started after her. He climbed into his car, put it in reverse, punched the control that closed the gate, glanced in the mirror—and saw Alex, setting off through the trees toward the adjoining property.

"Holy hell," he muttered. He left the car in the driveway and went after her. "Where do you think you're going now?" he snapped, when he caught her.

"The same place I was going before you interfered. Home."

Travis let go of her, folded his arms across his chest and

smirked. "Yeah, well, first you'd have to scale the ten-foot wall that separates my property from the place next door."

"I'll manage."

"I doubt it. Besides, you really have led a sheltered life, Ms. Thorpe, if you don't realize your mausoleum is at least an hour's drive from here."

"It is not a mausoleum." Her tone was frigid. "And I never had any intention of walking. I'll call for a cab, just as soon as I find a pay phone."

"Listen, lady, you want to go home?" Travis slapped his hands on his hips. "Fine. I'll drive you there."

"I don't need you to do anything for me, thank you very much. I am perfectly capable of—"

Hell. "Look, this is crazy," Travis said, and shoved a hand through his hair.

"It is not crazy. There must be a hundred public phones on that road."

"I don't mean that, dammit. I mean—I mean, what happened this morning."

"I have no idea what you're talking about."

Alex turned on her heel and began walking toward the gate. Travis stepped out in front of her, clasped her shoulders and stopped her.

"Let's not play games, Princess. You know exactly what I'm talking about. Things were going fine until I—until—"

"Until?"

He took a deep, deep breath. "Until I lied."

Alex blinked. "Lied?"

"I didn't have an appointment." He took another breath, dragging it deep into his lungs as if it might be his last, and glared at her. "I just—I panicked."

"Panicked?"

"Do you think you could stop repeating everything I say?"

He folded his arms again. She wished he hadn't. It made her look, really look, at that broad expanse of tanned, muscled chest; at those rounded biceps. At the swirl of dark hair that tapered to a silken line before disappearing into the unbuttoned waistband of his jeans.

She forced her gaze to his face. "I'm not repeating everything you…" She stopped, bit her lip, cleared her throat. "I don't know what you're talking about, Travis. Panicked about what?"

He turned and started walking. She hesitated, then followed him past the house, through a small garden and down to the beach. When they reached the sand, he turned and looked at her. "You're not the first woman who spent the night in my bed," he said gruffly.

Alex nodded. His words sent a funny little pain through her breast but she ignored it.

"There's no need to boast," she said coolly. "I didn't think I was."

"Yeah, well, I just want to be sure you understand that."

She kicked off her shoes and dug her toes into the warm sand. "You needn't hammer it in. There was nothing special about last night. I've got that."

"No. No, you don't!" He caught hold of her wrists and yanked her toward him. "There damned well *was* something special about last night, and you know it."

A gust of wind blew Alex's hair across her face. She tugged one hand free, scooped back the strand and stared at him, bewildered.

"Then why—I mean, what—"

"I told you. I panicked." His scowl deepened. "Listen, you think it's easy for me to say this, Princess? I'll tell you right now, it's not."

"To say what? I don't have a clue what you're talking about."

"I have no intention of getting into any kind of permanent relationship here. I told you that, straight out."

Her heart skipped a beat. Was he going to tell her he'd changed his mind? Not that she wanted him to. Those few seconds of craziness this morning, when she might have, were mercifully past.

"I know you did," she said carefully. "And I told you the same thing."

"Exactly. Still, there we were, planning our day together."

Alex looked even more confused. "Are you telling me you never spend the daylight hours with the women you sleep with?"

"Don't be ridiculous! Of course I do. It's just that—that..."

It's just that what, Baron? That you never really wanted to, until now? That the thought of teaching this woman to handle a fast car, or to eat chili dogs and ride roller coasters, gives you more pleasure than anything you've done in your entire life?

Panic swept over him, like a rogue wave rolling in across the ocean and threatening to forever change the landscape.

"It's just that I didn't want to have to hurt you by telling you not to get the wrong idea."

"About what?"

Why was she making this so difficult?

"About something happening here. Between us, I mean. Because—because it isn't."

"My oh my," Alex said sweetly. "You do think a lot of yourself, Cowboy."

"I want to go on seeing you, Alex." A muscle knotted in his cheek. "But I'm not going to put down stakes, or roots, or whatever it is women want me to put down. Is that clear?"

Alex raised one eyebrow. "Excuse me," she said coolly, "but I don't recall exhibiting any interest in you as a gardener."

"You know what I mean."

"I do, indeed. And didn't you hear me make a similar statement just yesterday?"

"Yeah." The muscle in his cheek danced again. "But that didn't stop you from going along with the plans I was making for today."

Alex laughed. "I don't know which is worse, Travis, your oversize ego or your lamebrained way of looking at things." She stepped forward, her smile turning into a scowl, her index finger aimed at the center of his chest. "*You* made the plans. *I* went along with them out of politeness. Do you really think that means I was trying to dig a hole for those roots you don't want to plant?"

Two bands of red feathered along his cheekbones.

"I didn't say that, exactly."

"No?" Alex flashed her brightest smile. "What *did* you say, exactly?"

"Just that—that we don't want to let this thing get out of hand."

"Our affair, you mean."

"Yes. Our—our…" Why was the word so hard to say? The Princess wasn't having a problem with it. She wasn't having a problem with any of this. She was ready, willing and downright eager to have the kind of easy come, easy go relationship he always wanted with a woman and rarely found—in which case, why was he feeling so damned ticked off? "Our affair," he said, finally.

She nodded her agreement, but a sudden weariness seemed to settle over her. All she wanted to do was go home, take a long, hot bath and try to get her life back on track. Because it wasn't on track; it hadn't been, since the night of the auction.

"Actually," she said softly. "Actually, I think—I think we should end this."

"End what?"

"This—whatever you want to call this relation—"

She gasped as Travis hauled her into his arms and crushed her mouth under his.

"It'll be over when it's over," he whispered, against her lips. "You got that, Princess?"

She knew the right thing to do was tell him that she didn't take orders from men anymore, especially ones who were arrogant, egocentric and unremittingly macho…but his mouth was on hers again, his arms held her tight, and, with a soft moan of surrender, she gave herself up to the kiss.

After a long time, he lifted his head and smiled.

"Now," he said smugly, "how about lesson number one on the Porsche?"

Alex frowned. "But you said—"

"Yeah, but we straightened all that out." He grinned. "So, what do you say? You want to take the wheel or not?"

Tell him no, Alex thought. Say, thank you, Travis, but you were right. We should maintain our perspective, keep some distance. After all, she'd spent yesterday with him, and the day before. Did she want to be with him, again?

"Princess?"

She looked up into those deep green eyes and her heart turned over.

"I'd love to," she said, and he smiled.

Alex stepped on the pedal as Travis's car flew up toward the lip of Eagle Canyon.

"Easy," Travis said. "Princess, hey, slow down, will you? Those look like some pretty tight turns up ahead." He groaned, pretended to shut his eyes as she laughed and whipped through them. "Lord, I've created a monster!"

"Oh, damn."

"What?"

"The gate's just ahead, and it's closed. I'll have to stop and punch in the code."

"Thank goodness," Travis breathed, but he was grinning.

Once through the gate, Alex accelerated again. She brought the car to a squealing stop in front of Thorpe House and turned toward Travis.

"Well?"

He looked at her. They'd driven with the windows open and the wind had tousled her hair. He hadn't given her time to put on any makeup, so the color in her face came from excitement. And she was wearing an old T-shirt of his along with a washed out pair of his jeans, the cuffs rolled to mid-calf. She was, in other words, a rumpled mess...and she was so beautiful that it made him ache just to see her.

"Travis?" She laughed and tossed back a strand of hair that had fallen over her cheek. "Don't tell me my driving was so awful that it left you speechless!"

"Well," he said, "I don't think Michael Andretti has anything to worry about, just yet..." He grinned when she made a face. "Okay, okay. The truth is, you weren't bad."

"The truth is, I was terrific!"

"Yeah, you were pretty good."

"I was great!"

Travis laughed, leaned forward and brushed his mouth lightly over hers. "Another couple of lessons, you'll be ready to go out and buy yourself a red convertible."

They smiled at each other and then Alex cleared her throat. "Well..."

"Well."

"Thank you for a wonderful day."

"You're welcome." He curved his hand around her jaw, bent to her and kissed her again, lingering over the shape and taste of her mouth. "I'll call you tomorrow."

"No," she said quickly. "I, ah, I have things to do tomorrow."

He drew back and smiled politely. "Of course. Actually, so have I. How about dinner tomorrow evening?"

"Call me," she said brightly. "And we'll see."

She reached for the door and he reached for her, the pressure of his hand viselike. "Don't play games with me, Alex."

She looked at him. "Games?"

"And don't play dumb, either. I told you yesterday, I don't share."

"Yes." Her smile was quick. "Yes, you did. While it lasts, you said, you'll be faithful to me."

"And I expect the same of you."

"Certainly. It's just that I do have a life of my own,

Travis. You reminded me of that this morning. And I'm glad you did.''

His eyes darkened. "You mean that, don't you."

It wasn't a question, not the way he said it. But she *did* mean it. Of course, she meant it...

A lump formed in her throat. She swallowed once, twice, then pasted a smile to her lips.

"Yes. Yes, I do. I told you, Travis, I want to enjoy my freedom.''

"Fine." The muscle in his cheek ticked as he slid behind the wheel, then slammed the door. "I'll pick you up at seven tomorrow evening.''

"But I asked you to call me first.''

Her protest came too late. Travis had already put the car in gear and roared away. She stood looking after him until nothing remained but plumes of dust. Then she sighed and climbed the steps to the house.

He came for her, every evening. Drove her home, in the small hours of each following morning, as if they'd never discussed not spending all their time together. They were together weekends, too, at Malibu—except for the weekend they flew up to the Napa Valley and walked the vineyards at Peregrine.

"I've given my approval to the sale," Alex said, as they sat on the steps of the veranda of the big Victorian house on the hill. "You can tell your father Peregrine is his, whenever he wants it.''

"Fine," Travis said, lifting her fingers to his lips. He smiled at her, rose to his feet and tugged her up beside him. "I made reservations at that inn on the coast.''

"Mmm." Alex winced.

"What's the matter, Princess?"

"Headache," she said, then smiled. "I'll be fine, as soon as we reach the inn. Staying there sounds wonderful.''

It would have been, but by early evening, she felt exhausted. By nightfall, her teeth were chattering and her bones ached. And by morning, she had a fever of 102.

Over her protests, Travis phoned for a doctor.

"Flu," the doctor said matter-of-factly. "It's going around. She needs rest, plenty of liquids, aspirin…"

Alex moaned, sat up and tried to get out of bed. Travis put his arm around her.

"Going to be sick," she whimpered.

"Not without me," he said, and carried her to the bathroom.

To her dismay, he stayed with her, supported her while she retched, gently wiped her face with a cool, wet cloth and carried her back to bed.

"As I was saying," the doctor continued, "she needs rest, liquids, aspirin for the fever, light foods when her stomach can hold them, She'll be fine in a few days."

Travis looked at Alex. "What can I do to make you feel better, darlin'?"

"You can take me home," she whispered. "As nice as this place is, I'd really rather be sick in familiar surroundings."

Travis looked at the doctor. "We live in Malibu, but we came by plane. Can I fly her home?"

"I don't live in Malibu," Alex said wearily, "I live in—"

"Sure," the doctor said. "I'll give her something to control the nausea, you get that fever down with the aspirin, wrap her up in blankets, and you can take her to Malibu."

"But I don't live in—"

"Shut up," Travis said gently, and then he smiled and shook the doctor's hand. "Thanks, Doc."

"No problem." The doctor grinned. "Just be sure and take a bucket with you, just in case."

Alex said she felt like a Red Cross package.

Travis said she looked like a disaster area.

But he said it tenderly, as he strapped her into the seat

beside him in the Comanche. She did, too. Her face was pale, her eyes huge and dark. Her hair was lank, after two days without shampooing, and the bucket she held clutched in her lap didn't do much to improve the picture.

She looked tired and ill and fragile, and in that moment, he knew that he felt something for this woman he had never felt before.

It scared the hell out of him.

"What?" she said, as a furrow appeared between his eyes.

"Nothing," he said briskly, and turned his attention to the plane.

She was sick for five days.

She threw up. She sweated. She moaned. She shivered.

And Travis took care of her.

He held her head when she was sick, bathed her when she was hot. He soothed her when she moaned and warmed her with his body when she shivered. And then, on the morning of the sixth day, Alex woke up, stretched, yawned—and announced that she could eat a horse.

Travis sat up, too. "Does that mean you're feeling better?" he said, with a hopeful smile.

She grinned. "I feel wonderful." Her grin faded. "Were you here, all the time? Or did I dream it?"

"Well," he said modestly, "not all the time. I took five minutes off, every now and then, for things like showering and making coffee."

"Yes, but you were with me all the rest of the time." Her eyes met his. "You didn't have to do it, you know. You could have taken me home. I have a housekeeper."

His smile tilted. He cupped her face, smoothed her hair back from her temples and kissed the tip of her nose.

"Yes," he said softly. "I know."

The look on his face was gentle, as was the touch of his hands, and the warmth of his smile made her want to lean into his arms and cling to him—cling to him, forever—

proof, surely, that she was still under the weather. Otherwise, she'd never have wanted such a thing.

"I wanted to take care of you, Princess. It's as simple as that."

Alex nodded gravely. "Thank you."

Their eyes met, their glances held. Travis wanted to gather her into his arms, hold her, tell her—tell her...

Instead, he cleared his throat. "There's nothing to thank me for," he said lightly. "Just be sure and put me in for the Nobel Prize and we'll call it an even trade."

She laughed—until she looked past him and glimpsed herself in the mirror. "Oh my goodness! Is that me?"

"Is what you?"

"That—that creature I see in the mirror. Whoa. What a mess!"

Travis leaped for her as she flung back the covers. "Hey. Not so fast, darlin'. You're liable to fall on your face."

"We'll all fall on our faces, if I don't get hold of some soap and water." She rose from the bed, wrapping the sheet around herself. She knew it was silly to be so modest now but this had nothing to do with modesty and everything to do with the sudden realization that something had changed between them. "Travis? If you could just lend me something to wear, until I get home...?"

A funny look came and went on his face, so quickly that she thought she'd imagined it.

"Sure." He rose from the bed and came toward her. "After we shower, I'll lay out something for you to put on."

"No. I mean—I mean, I think I'd better shower alone." She managed a quick smile. "I've got lots of secret little feminine things to do, after all. Wash my hair. Shave my legs..."

Travis eyed her warily and then he nodded. "Okay. But if you feel the least bit woozy—"

"I'll yell, I promise."

The shower felt wonderful. Alex stood under the stream, eyes closed, soaping, shampooing, scrubbing and rinsing until she felt clean. Images came and went: Travis, holding her. Helping her. Urging her to drink cool juices.

I wanted to take care of you, Princess. It's as simple as that.

Her lover had become her friend. For some reason, the thought was as frightening as it was exhilarating.

"Princess?"

She took a breath, shut off the water and cracked open the shower door. Travis stood outside—at least, she thought, as she began to laugh, an enormous white towel stood outside, with a man's denim-clad legs peeping out from under it.

She stepped onto the mat and let him enfold her in the towel.

"Mmm," she sighed, as he drew her close, "that feels lovely."

Travis nodded. "Yeah," he said, and sternly warned his body to behave itself. Alex had been ill. She was still fragile—and heaven only knew how she'd react, when she saw what he'd done. He wrapped the towel snugly around her, stepped back and motioned her ahead of him, into the bedroom. "Well," he said briskly, "I've laid out something for you to wear. If it's not what you want, just tell me."

She laughed as she padded across the carpet. "Anything that makes me look human again will be just…" Her words trailed away as she looked at the clothing on the bed. A pair of her jeans. One of her silk blouses. Panties that were hers, and a bra. She looked up. Travis was at the closet, his back to her. "Oh, Travis," she said, and smiled. "That was sweet of you."

He didn't turn around. "What was?"

"Going to my house and picking up some stuff for me to wear. That was really—"

He swung toward her. "I picked up everything," he said gruffly.

Alex cocked her head. "I don't understand."

"Well, maybe not everything, but most of what was in

your closet and in your dresser drawers. Your housekeeper collected the things she thought you'd want and I brought them here, but we'll go back, if I forgot anything, and—''

He looked at her puzzled face, fell silent and stepped aside. Alex stared past him, into the closet, where her clothing hung side by side with his.

"Travis?" Her gaze flew to his. "What is this?"

"You're moving in with me."

"Moving...?" Alex laughed. "No, I'm not. I have a house. A life. And we agreed—''

"Nothing's changed." His voice was rough and so was the way he reached for her and enclosed her in his arms. "It's crazy, not living together."

"But we agreed—''

"I know all about that. But while we're together—''

"While it lasts, you mean."

He nodded, his green eyes on hers. "Yeah. While it does, I want you with me."

Alex bristled. "Did it ever occur to you to ask what *I* might want, Cowboy?"

His hands covered hers. Gently, persistently, he drew the towel from her fingers and let it fall to the floor so she stood within his embrace, naked.

"All right. I'm asking, Princess. Do you want to be with me, or don't you?"

She looked up at him, knowing what her answer should be, knowing she should demand her independence, that there was no way she ought to let him take control of her life—or of her heart.

He bent his head, kissed her. "I'm waiting," he whispered.

Alex's arm curled around Travis's neck. "This is crazy."

It was all the answer he needed.

He stepped out of his jeans and drew her down to the bed, into his arms. He rained kisses on her temples, on her throat. He licked her nipples, bit them gently, stroked her thighs and buried his face between them.

It had been so long. Days, an eternity...

"My turn," she said softly, and knelt over him, kissing her way down his hard-muscled body, taking him into her mouth, loving him with teeth and tongue until he groaned and rolled her beneath him. He entered her on one hard, possessive stroke and she burst instantly into a million shards of light.

"My beautiful Princess," Travis whispered, as he settled her in his arms.

Alex nestled against him, closed her eyes and told herself it just wasn't true...

But it was.

She'd fallen in love with Travis.

CHAPTER TWELVE

TRAVIS had never been so happy.

And it amazed him.

Even at the beginning of his marriage to Cathy, before things had started to go bad between them, there'd been mornings it had seemed a chore to smile and be cheerful. He'd had something about work on his mind, or sometimes just Cathy's early-morning chatter had made his teeth grind together.

Alex was different.

She woke him with kisses, or he woke her. It didn't much matter. Either way, by the time he left the bed, he was always smiling. He'd never much cared for breakfast and he still didn't, but having coffee across from his Princess's lovely face seemed the perfect way to begin the day. Ending it by knowing she'd be at the door to greet him was even more perfect. It was amazing, how fast he came to expect to see her there, waiting for him. And she always was, despite her growing involvement in the empire her father had left her.

Oh, yeah. He was happy. And everybody knew it. Some, like Pete Haskell, teased him unmercifully.

"What's with you, Baron?" Pete kept asking. "That grin stuck on your face, or what?"

And Travis would chuckle and say, yeah, it probably was.

He knew Alex was happy, too, though there were some moments that happiness was put to the test. Like the time the phone rang, early one morning, and she reached across him to pick it up when he didn't hear it.

He woke up just as she said "hello" in a sleepy voice.

"Who is it?" he asked, but he knew it was trouble as he watched the expression on her face.

"Yes," she said coldly, "this is 555-0937." And then she thrust the phone at him, sat back against the pillows and glared.

Travis sat up. "Yeah?" he growled. "Oh. Right. Uh-huh. Sure. That's great, Emma. Thanks for calling." He put the phone back on the nightstand and reached for Alex, but she had slipped from the bed. "That was Emma," he said.

"Indeed," Alex said pleasantly. She put on her robe and went into the bathroom. When she returned, Travis was lying back against the pillows.

"She's my secretary."

"Did I ask?"

"You didn't have to."

"It's a free country, Travis. You don't have to—"

"But I do." He sat up. She looked at that expanse of tanned chest and muscle, swallowed dryly and looked away. "Dammit, Alex, do you really think I'd cheat on you?"

"No."

"Then, what was that all about?"

Alex picked up her brush and stroked it through her hair. "We have an agreement," she said calmly. "No sleeping with anybody else while we're together. Isn't that right?"

She looked at his reflection in the mirror, saw his mouth thin. "Is that why you think I wouldn't cheat on you?" he said gruffly. "Because we made some agreement?"

"I just wondered," she said, deciding to ignore the question, "whether your secretary knows who I am."

Travis could feel a headache starting just behind his eyes. "I don't know."

"She didn't seem to. I mean, she sounded surprised to hear my voice."

"I guess she was." He sat up, tossed the blanket aside, got to his feet and walked to the bathroom. "I'm not in the habit of discussing my private life with my secretary."

"Who do you discuss it with, then?"

He came out of the bathroom, still naked, and stood just behind her. "Listen," he said carefully, "I'm not very good at games, first thing in the morning. If you want to tell me something, just say it, okay?''

Alex hesitated. She wasn't very good at games, anytime of day. What was wrong with her this morning? She'd answered the telephone, Travis's secretary had seemed startled to hear her voice. On the face of it, there was nothing to be upset about. On the contrary. It was nice to know that the women who danced in and out of his life either didn't spend the night with him very often or didn't feel secure enough to answer the phone.

Except, that didn't change the fact that she was just another one of those faceless women. Oh, she might last a little longer. He might even feel a twinge of regret when their affair ended but end it would. She'd gone into this, knowing that. Knowing, too, that Travis wouldn't really make her part of his life. He'd never introduce her to his family, or to the people he worked with. Not even his secretary would know she existed.

"Princess?"

Alex swallowed, lifted her gaze to the mirror and managed a smile.

"Sorry. I—I just…I woke up with a headache this morning, that's all."

Travis smiled, put his arms around her and drew her back against him. "Me, too," he said softly. "And I know just the cure."

"No." Her voice was sharp, and she puffed out a breath and tried again. "No, really, Travis. What I need are a couple of aspirin." Their eyes met in the mirror, his narrowed, hers shadowed. "Okay?"

He went on looking at her for what seemed a long time. Then he shrugged and his arms dropped to his sides.

"Sure. I have to get going, anyway. Emma called to tell me a client wants to see me pronto." He moved toward the bathroom again, then paused in the doorway. "Alex?"

"Yes?"

He hesitated, and then he cleared his throat. "How about meeting me in town for dinner?"

She nodded. She'd done that before, driving in—she had a red Miata convertible, now—parking in the garage near his office and waiting for him in the lobby.

"What time shall I be there?"

"How about a little before five?" He cleared his throat again. "Come up to my office, and I'll introduce you around."

Her heart did a funny little stumble-step. "Fine," she said, as if this wasn't the very first time he'd even hinted at letting her into his world.

Travis nodded. "Fine," he repeated—and told himself it really would be.

She dressed as carefully as if she were going to the board meeting of one of the corporations her father had left her, and arrived so early that she had to drive around the block for a few minutes, to kill time.

By the time she'd ridden the elevator to Travis's floor and made her way down the corridor to his office, her heart was pounding.

His secretary—Emma—greeted her with a smile.

"You must be Ms. Thorpe." She rose and extended her hand. "Mr. Baron is taking a last-minute call. Won't you sit down?"

"Thank you," Alex said politely.

She sat, picked up a magazine, made a show of thumbing through it. She looked up, met the secretary's curious gaze. The woman blushed, smiled and busied herself with something on her desk. Questions tumbled through Alex's head.

Had Emma recognized her voice? She'd known Alex's name, but what did that mean? What had Travis told her? That an Alexandra Thorpe would be stopping by? Or had he told her more? What? What would he tell her? That they lived together? How did you say something like that? What did you call a woman who lived with a man? Calling her his "date" was just plain silly but referring to her as his lover was far too intimate. Did you call her his mistress? No. A man supported his mistress. Paid her rent. Bought her clothes. Travis did none of that for her. She'd never have let him, even if she didn't have her own money. Being a mistress was completely, totally demeaning.

"Princess."

Alex shot to her feet. Travis stood in the open door to his private office. The obvious pleasure in his smile and in the way he'd spoken the name he used for her—their own, private name—put her at ease.

She smiled and came toward him, chastising herself for having had such foolish thoughts.

"Travis," she said softly.

He smiled, too, and held out his hands.

"Whoops. Sorry, Baron. I didn't know you had company."

Alex swung around. A man smiled at her from the doorway to the outer office.

"Pete." Travis frowned. "Pete, I thought you were out of town this week."

"I was, but I got back sooner than…" Pete Haskell's smile became a grin. "Wow." He hurried forward and took Alex's hand. "You're Alexandra Thorpe."

"Listen," Travis said quickly, "I'm kind of busy right now, so—"

Alex smiled slightly. "Why, yes. Have we met?"

"Not really." Haskell chuckled. "But I wish we had, that night at the bachelor thing. The auction."

Color flooded her face. "Oh."

"Yeah." Haskell winked at Travis. "Oh, indeed. You didn't tell us you were seeing Miss Thorpe, Baron."

Travis's face looked as if it had been chiseled from granite. "I don't tell you lots of things, Haskell."

"So, what's the deal? Has this been going on long?"

Alex knew her face was burning. She looked at Travis. "Has what been going on long?" he said coldly.

"You know. This. Are you guys dating, or what?"

Or what, Alex thought, and bit back a hysterical laugh.

Travis put his arm around Alex's waist. "We're late," he said, and led her past Haskell, past his secretary, and out the door. He didn't speak again until they were in the elevator. "I'm sorry about that, Princess. Haskell's a jerk."

"I thought you didn't discuss your private life at the office," Alex said stiffly.

"I don't."

"But the auction must have been quite a topic of conversation."

Travis sighed. "Yeah, it was. But the auction wasn't exactly personal."

"What happened between us was."

"Of course. I didn't mean—"

The elevator stopped. The doors opened and a gentleman with white hair and rheumy eyes stepped into the car. Travis bit back a groan.

"Travis," the man said pleasantly.

Travis nodded.

"And who is this lovely young lady?" Old man Sullivan smiled, took Alex's hand and lifted it to his lips.

"Her name is Alexandra," Travis mumbled.

"A charming name for a charming..." Sullivan pursed his lips. "Alexandra? Alexandra. Why is that name so familiar?"

The elevator stopped again. The doors whisked open. Travis grasped Alex's hand and hurried her into the lobby.

"See you tomorrow, John," he called.

Alex kept a stony silence until he steered her into a quiet corner. Then she rounded on Travis, eyes flashing, and slapped her hands on her hips.

"Everyone in that awful placc knows about me," she hissed.

"Princess—"

"Don't you 'Princess' me, Cowboy!" She glared at him. "What more do they know, huh? Besides the fact that I made a fool of myself, bidding on you."

"Nothing. What could they know, other than that?"

Her eyes narrowed. "Other than that I made a fool of myself, you mean?"

"No. Yes. Hell, Alex, you're the one who said it, not me!" Travis looked around. "Do we have to discuss this here? I mean, couldn't we pick someplace a little more, uh, more discreet?"

"I want an answer to my question first. What else did you tell all these people about me?" She took a deep breath. "Did you tell them what happened—what we did that night? What I—what I…"

"Dammit, Alex!" Travis grabbed her elbow and yanked her toward him, his face dark. "What kind of man do you think I am? No, I did not tell them what happened. I told you, I don't discuss my private life—"

"At work. Yes, so you said. So, how come everybody leered at me?"

"Lord!" Travis shoved his hand through his hair. "They didn't leer. They were just curious, that's all. You can hardly blame them. I mean, yeah, sure, they probably do remember that you, uh, that you made that bid at the auction. And now that they know we're dating…"

He knew he'd made a mistake as soon as the word left his mouth, but it was too late. Alex's lovely face went white.

"Dating," she said, very softly.

"Yeah." He cleared his throat. "Well, we are—kind of."

"Dating," she said again. "You and I are dating."

"Alex…"

She wrenched free of his hand, turned on her heel and marched away from him. Travis cursed and went after her, but he got caught up in a crowd at the exit door. By the time he reached the street, she was gone, but where?

He had no idea.

He drove to Malibu. She wasn't there. He drove to Thorpe House. She wasn't there, either. By ten that night, he'd put what seemed like a million miles on the car but he still hadn't found her.

He was furious and worried. Mostly furious—okay, mostly

worried. Where could she have gone? And what was she so angry about, anyway? Travis sat on the deck of his beach house, the phone, a glass, and a half-empty bottle of good California Merlot on the table beside him, and glared out at the sea.

What did women want from men besides the chance to drive them nuts?

"What was I supposed to do?" he demanded of the night. "She was mad because I'd never introduced her to anybody at my office. And then, when I did, she got mad because they figured out how we'd met."

Travis poured more wine into his glass and drank it.

Women were crazy. There was no pleasing them. He'd asked Alex to move in with him. Wasn't that enough? He'd never asked a woman to live with him before, never. Not before his marriage, certainly not after.

"Dammit," he growled, picked up the phone and hit the speed-dial button for Slade's Boston number.

Slade answered on the first ring. "Hello," he snarled, "and whoever this is, I'll tell you right now, I'm not in the mood for chitchat."

"Well, neither am I," Travis snarled back.

"Trav?" Slade's voice softened a little. "Hey, man. How'd you know I needed to—"

"Tell me something," Travis said. "What the hell is the matter with the female of the species?"

Slade gave a choked laugh. "The fact that they *are* female. That's what's the matter with them!"

"Yeah." Travis stood up and walked down the wooden steps to the sandy beach. "There's this woman."

"There always is."

"I asked her to move in with me."

"You what? Listen, man, before you do anything serious, stop and think."

"It isn't serious. I mean, okay, it's serious now. But it won't be serious forever. We have an understanding. We stay together, no strings, no commitments—" Travis took the phone from his ear and glared at it. "Damn you, kid, stop laughing!"

"They all want commitments," Slade said, and then he cleared his throat. "At least, they want them when they want them, not when you get around to making them."

Travis frowned. "What are you talking about?"

"Nothing, man, nothing at all. Look, about this babe—"

"She's not a 'babe,'" Travis said coldly. "Her name is Alexandra."

"Alexandra, huh? Pretty classy name for a... Wait a second. The babe—the woman who bought you at that auction. Wasn't her name—"

"What if it was?"

"Hey, there's no need to get defensive. I'm just surprised, that's all. I mean, the lady bought you for hot times—"

"Watch how you talk about her, Slade."

Slade sighed. "Listen, man, all I'm saying is that it's, uh, sort of unusual that she's become your mistress."

"She's not my mistress."

"What would you call her, then? If she's living in your house?"

Travis opened his mouth, then shut it. He raked his fingers through his hair.

"I don't know what I'd call her," he said. "Hell, that's part of the problem. She's—she's got to be called something, you know what I mean? When I introduce her to people."

"She has a name, right? So just use it."

"No. That's not the point. We're living together, Slade. How do I let people know that?"

"Why should they have to know it?" Slade asked reasonably.

Travis frowned. "Well—well, because she doesn't want to be some kind of secret. You know, as if she doesn't have a real function in my life."

"Trav, man, you are in deep trouble, do you know that?"

Travis sighed. "I just need to call her something, kid."

"Your date?"

"Hell, no."

"Your lover, then."

"No, she'd never go for that."

"How about introducing her as your friend?"

Travis laughed.

"Well then, the only thing that leaves is that she's your mistress."

Travis shook his head. "She's not. Or maybe she is. The thing is, she's more than a mistress."

"Well, tell her that."

"Yeah?" Travis thought about it. "Yeah," he said slowly, and smiled. "Maybe she'd like to hear that. 'Princess,' I could say, 'Alex, I just want you to know that you're more than a mistress to me...'"

"You son of a bitch!"

He swung around just in time to see Alex's fist blur through the air. She caught him on the chin. He rocked back on his heels, and the phone fell from his hand.

"Princess," he said. "Princess, what...?"

"I am not your mistress, Travis Baron."

"I know." Bewildered, he rubbed his aching jaw. "I said that. You're so much more—"

"You know something, Cowboy? You're a grade-A idiot."

She turned and ran. Travis started after her but he tripped on the phone. By the time he got to the driveway, she was behind the wheel of the Miata.

"Alex," he yelled.

Alex stuck out her arm. Something shiny dangled from her fingertips.

"No," Travis said, *"nooo..."*

The keys she'd taken from the Porsche arced through the moonlit night and landed in the heavy shrubbery that lined the driveway.

The Miata's engine roared and the car shot forward.

"Alex," he shouted, but she didn't even look back. Travis

set his jaw. Okay, enough was enough. She wanted to leave him? Let her.

He sat just at the place where the waves came in and kissed the sand. The phone was back in his pocket, and what remained of the wine was in his glass. He let the cold water curl over his toes while he told himself it was just as well it was over.

Their affair had grown far too complicated. Besides, it would have ended anyway, sooner or later.

Alexandra Thorpe was only a woman. A beautiful woman, sure, but beautiful women were as common in southern California as sand on the beach.

Okay, so she was bright, too. And she had a nice sense of fun. Yeah, and he liked that spirit of hers, he thought ruefully, wincing as he rubbed his chin. And she had a love for life that made each day a joy. He could talk with her, too, about everything, the big stuff and the small. Well, so what? She was still just another woman…

The phone rang. He yanked it from his pocket, heart pounding, put it to his ear—and heard his brother Gage's voice.

Gage sounded bad. Bad enough so that, just for a second, Travis forgot his own troubles.

"Gage? What's the matter, man? You sound—"

"Listen, Trav, I, ah, I just wanted to ask you a question."

"Yeah? Gage, you sure you're okay? You sound—"

"I'm trying to talk quietly, dammit! I don't want Natalie to hear."

"Oh." Travis cleared his throat. "What's up?"

"Well…" Gage cleared his throat, too. "Listen, when one person wants a divorce but the other person doesn't…"

Travis's shoulders slumped as he listened. Gage and Natalie's divorce was still on, even though Gage didn't want it. Well, that was typical, wasn't it? When a woman got a damned fool idea in her head, a man was doomed no matter what he said or did.

"Trav," Gage said, "I know I'm not making sense but this is all so confusing."

"Love, you mean." Travis laughed. "Yeah, it sure is."

"Look, I know you don't understand. I mean, I know you're not in love, that you've never really been in love..."

"Love sucks, man." Travis's voice roughened. "A man loses his equilibrium, turns into some jackass he doesn't recognize. And for what? All so a woman can drive him crazy, turn him into a—a gibbering idiot."

"Trav? Are you okay?"

"Yeah. I'm fine."

"You sure? You don't sound okay."

"Listen, Gage, I'm—I'm kind of in the middle of something here. You want to know if you can stop Natalie from going through with this divorce? The answer is no, pal. I'm sorry to tell you this but, if she wants out, she's out."

Gage nodded. "Yeah. I kind of figured..." He blew out a breath. "Thanks anyway."

"Gage? Don't let her go. Don't ever let the woman you love go, not if you have to turn cartwheels to keep her..."

The woman you love.

The phone fell from Travis's hand. The woman you love. That was Alex. He loved her. Yes, he loved her. This was no affair that would end; it was forever...

Unless he let her go.

"Baron," he said aloud, "she was right. You really are an idiot."

Travis leaped to his feet and ran for the house. Halfway there, he stopped, raced back, grabbed the phone and punched in Slade's Boston number.

"Listen kid," he said, when his brother answered, "Gage is having a bad time."

Slade laughed. "Yeah. There's a lot of that going around lately."

"Just call him, okay? He isn't home but I got his number from my caller ID box. Take it down."

"Trav?" Slade cleared his throat. "Listen man, actually—actually, this isn't the best—"

"Tell him not to be an idiot, okay? No man should ever let a woman he loves get away from him."

"Love," Slade growled, "love? Who even knows what the word means?"

Travis banged open the door to the beach house. "You'll know," he said gruffly, "believe me, kid, when it happens, you'll know."

Slade said something, but Travis didn't wait to hear what it was. He hit the disconnect button, dumped the phone on the table, and began looking for his extra set of keys. Where in hell were they?

In the drawer, right where he'd put them the day he'd first bought the car.

He paused just long enough to glug down a cup of instant coffee and to leave a message on his answering machine.

"Alex," he said, "if this is you calling…just tell me where you are and stay there. You hear me, Princess? Stay there."

Except he was pretty sure he knew where she was, and that was where he was going, right now.

CHAPTER THIRTEEN

ALEX was exhausted by the time she reached the big Victorian house at Peregrine Vineyards in the Napa Valley.

And she was still furious, though she'd worked off some of her anger by taking every steep and tight curve on the way as if she'd driven them all her life.

Fantastic, she thought coldly, as she brought the car to a stand-on-the-brakes, skidding stop in the driveway. She'd had a red-hot affair with Travis Baron and all she had to show for it was a newfound talent for driving like a speed demon.

So much for finding herself as a woman.

Thunder rumbled across the valley, as if to underscore the thought. Alex grabbed her overnight bag from the seat beside her and ran for the house, just as the rain began.

"Great," she muttered, as she unlocked the door, then slammed it behind her.

A storm was just what she needed tonight. Sound and fury, courtesy of Mother Nature, to match the rage building inside her.

She tossed her car keys on the table, switched on the light and looked around. The house had looked more welcoming by daylight than it did now but where else could she have gone? Not to Thorpe House. Travis had been right about that, at least. The miserable old house *was* a mausoleum. The sooner she sold it, the better.

Alex went to the stairs and looked up. It was awfully dark up there. She hesitated, then made a face.

"You're an independent woman now," she muttered. "Are the shadows at the top of the stairs going to turn your knees to jelly?"

Maybe, especially if the thunder and lightning rolling over the valley got any closer.

She laughed nervously, took a deep breath and went upstairs.

There were lots of bedrooms, some of them still furnished. She picked one at random and dumped her overnight bag on the bed. There wasn't much in the bag, just some toiletries she'd picked up at a supermarket, her old robe, jeans, underwear, a T-shirt and sneakers. No real clothes, though. How could there be, when nothing of hers remained at Thorpe House? Travis had taken all of it, emptied her closets and drawers the day *he* had decided she was going to live with him.

Had he asked her? No. Had he even thought about asking her?

"No," she said, and her mouth thinned.

Arrogant, egotistical, self-centered bastard! Oh, she was far, far better off without him.

She peeled off her silk suit and blouse, her panty hose and pumps, all the things she'd worn today to mark what she'd thought would be her introduction into Travis's real life.

From now on, the only "real life" she was interested in was her own. The last vestiges of the old Alexandra had fallen away early this evening, when she'd realized—thank heavens—that she didn't love Travis at all. She'd just needed to think she did to justify the fact that she was sleeping with him. The effect of living a conservative, tradition-bound existence didn't fade so easily.

It would, now. She was free at last, free of everything.

Free of Travis.

The shower worked, which was more than she'd hoped for. There was a scratchy stack of towels in a cupboard beside the sink. She dried off quickly, ran her fingers through her hair and slipped on her robe.

How pathetic, that she'd tried to convince herself she loved him. Sex. Good old, down-and-dirty sex, was what their relationship had been all about. It was time she accepted that.

A jagged slash of lightning arced past the bathroom window. Alex jumped as thunder roared overhead. If only the storm would pass. She'd be all right, though. The house was big and old and, okay, a bit spooky, but so long as the roof didn't leak and the lights didn't go out...

Even imagining such a thing had been a mistake. Lightning flashed again, and the house was plunged into darkness.

Alex swallowed hard. She moved carefully into the bedroom and waited. The lights would come on again in a minute...

They did.

"You see?" she said shakily, and laughed.

The lights had come on, and life was going to improve, now that she'd taken charge of her existence. She supposed she had Travis to thank for that. If today hadn't happened, if he hadn't told her she was more than a mistress, she'd probably have gone on living with him right up until the minute he decided it was time for a new playmate. Because that was all she'd been to him. A playmate. An attractive, intelligent, quick-learning toy.

Tears burned behind Alex's eyes but crying over Travis would be ridiculous. What was there to cry about?

"Nothing," she said gruffly, and wiped her eyes with the backs of her hands.

Not one pathetic little thing. She'd behaved like a fool but at least she had the satisfaction of knowing she'd ended the affair, not he. Maybe that wasn't much but it was better than nothing. Definitely, it was. And now that she was free of Travis, she had lots of plans to make.

Alex plopped down on the bed and crossed her legs under her. First thing, she'd sell Thorpe House. She'd buy a condo in Brentwood. Or a place at Huntington Beach. She could even move in here. Well, no. She'd already agreed to sell this place. Why would she want to live here, anyway? There wasn't even any real reason she'd come here tonight...

Thunder roared. Lightning sizzled. And the room went dark again.

Alex waited, but this time the lights stayed off. The darkness was impenetrable. It was like being encased in black velvet. She couldn't see a thing...but she could hear. A scratching at the window. A tap. A sigh.

"Stop it," she whispered.

It was a tree branch, at the window. Rain, on the roof. It was the wind she heard moaning, not a person...

Lightning tore the room apart. Alex screamed and ran for the door but where was the door? She couldn't see it. She didn't know this house at all. She needed light, but where would she find candles or a flashlight?

In the kitchen. That was where such things were kept, at Thorpe House. All she had to do was get there.

Carefully, hands outstretched, she made her way out of the bedroom and down the endless stairs. She opened a door and walked into a closet but, finally, she felt tile under her feet, felt the outline of a stove under her fingertips.

The walls were lined with cabinets. Blindly, she felt her way from one to the other, opening drawers, feeling around in them, trying not to think about the creepy-crawlies that might be lurking in these long unused places.

It had been silly, driving here. Los Angeles was filled with hotels. She could have stayed in one, or tolerated one more night at Thorpe House. Coming here had been pointless. It was only that she still owned this house, that it was empty...

That it was filled with memories.

Was that the reason she'd come? So she could immerse herself in remembrance of the day she'd come here to sell Peregrine to a faceless stranger and, instead, ended up in Travis's arms?

No, of course not. She was here because she'd needed to get away from L.A. and everything that was familiar. Travis wasn't the reason. She didn't love him. She'd slept with him, that was all. Surely, she was woman enough to come to grips with that.

Thunder roared again. The house shook in the grip of the storm. Where were those damned candles? What about a flashlight? There had to be one...

There was. Alex heaved a sigh of relief as her hand closed around it. Now if it would just work....

"Yes," she said happily, as a beam of light shot across the kitchen.

That was lots better. Some light. Some logic. Maybe even something to warm her bones. Wine. Surely, there'd be some here.

She searched the kitchen. The living room. The dining room. Perplexed, she stood in the foyer, trying to imagine where the wine, assuming there was some, would be kept. Her father, then Carl, had always kept spirits in the library.

She found the library easily enough. She'd missed it the first time but she came on it the second time, just off the living room. Actually, she thought as she shone the light around, actually, this was, as she'd always thought, a house with great possibilities. Too bad she'd agreed to sell it. Living here might be fun.

And she was due for some fun. Oh, it was good to be running her own life again instead of letting Travis do it for her.

That was how she'd ended up in this mess. She'd let him take over. He'd made arrangements, and she'd been stuck with them. If he'd asked her to move in with him the way any polite, civilized man would have done, she'd surely have said no. The arrogance of him, to have assumed she'd leap at the chance. Why would she have?

She was an attractive, capable, intelligent woman. She had no desire to tie herself to one man. She had interests. An income. A veritable empire to look after. She didn't need a man to mess around in her life and tell her what to do, certainly not one like Travis, who'd thought nothing of organizing her existence as if she were incapable of making her own choices.

Alex stood in the center of the library and shone the flash-light beam into each dark corner. Aha! There was a built-in bar. And some bottles—admittedly dusty but so what? Didn't wine improve with age?

Fine. She'd stay here until the lights came on again. Of all the rooms in the house, this one was the coziest—if you could call mahogany-paneled walls, overstuffed sofas, a desk the size of a baseball field and acres of leather-bound books cozy.

She padded to the bar, tucked the flashlight under her arm, checked over the bottles and selected a Cabernet Sauvignon with a Peregrine falcon on the label. She poured herself a healthy couple of inches. Then, light in one hand, glass in the other, she settled onto a bar stool.

No, she thought grimly, she had not appreciated having Travis commandeer her life but that was what he'd done, right from the beginning.

She took a sip of the wine.

He had swept her across that dance floor, the night they'd met, despite all her objections. He'd kissed her, in front of everybody. Come to her house, unasked, broken into it, forced himself on her...

The glass trembled in her hand.

"Oh, Alex," she whispered, "can't you at least be honest about that?"

He hadn't forced himself on her. She'd wanted him to make love to her but she'd lacked the courage to admit it, so she'd let him take the decision out of her hands.

And it had been wonderful. Even now, she could almost feel the touch of his mouth on hers. On her breasts. She could remember the excitement that had raced through her blood as he'd carried her up the stairs to the bedroom.

She set the glass down, carefully, on the bar.

Travis's kisses. His caresses. His body, hard against hers. Nothing had prepared her for the reality of making love with him. He'd known just how to please her. To make her cry out his name.

To make her lose her heart.

The wind moaned its sympathy. Alex frowned, lifted the glass, drank some wine and scolded herself for giving in to such self-serving, maudlin thoughts.

Rolling around in gloom and doom wasn't going to get her anywhere. Maybe it really had been a mistake to come here tonight. She might have done better to have sought out lights. People. Noise. She'd never liked the club scene—another of Carl's complaints—but she was a new woman now. Maybe the new Alex would enjoy some night life.

Okay. Tomorrow night, she'd go out. Alone. Women did that today. She'd drive to one of those restaurants she was always hearing about, order champagne, choose something unpronounceable from the menu. And she'd wear something sexy and feminine. Her white suit, maybe. Or that little black knit dress...

The heck she would.

The suit, the dress, everything she owned was back at the house in Malibu. She had no clothes left to speak of, thanks to Travis. He was *impossible!* What had given him the right to move her things into his house without asking her? Why hadn't it occurred to him that she might not have wanted to move in with him and give up her newfound freedom?

How could he have known she'd love living with him, sharing his days and nights? He certainly wouldn't know how heavy her heart was now, as she contemplated all the days and nights that lay ahead, without him.

"Oh, hell," she said weakly, and reached for the bottle.

The glass clinked as she poured herself more wine. Why not? It would make her unwind, get her tired enough to curl up on the sofa, get some sleep. Maybe she wouldn't dream about Travis, about how she would miss him...

"I hate you, Travis," she said.

Her voice wobbled, but it was true. She had to remember that. She didn't love him, she hated him. She'd even gone back to Malibu to tell him so, because she certainly didn't want him to think he'd left her wounded. And, okay, maybe to ask him a question.

Do I mean anything at all to you, Travis? she'd been going to ask.

As it turned out, he'd provided the answer without her having to ask the question. She *did* mean something to him. She was more than a mistress, he'd said earnestly, as if it were a compliment, given her that hurt-puppy look as if he couldn't imagine why his words hadn't turned her giddy with delight.

Alex gave a great, gulping sob. "I really, really despise you, Travis," she said, as the tears streamed down her face.

He'd let people think she was—whatever they thought she was. That smarmy man in the office. Oh, the way he'd looked at her, as if he knew some dirty joke and she were the punchline. And that other boor. The look in his piggy eyes when his tiny brain started piecing things together. Everybody had stared at her as if she were a one-night stand.

"And I wasn't," she whispered.

She wasn't. She'd been Travis's lover.

But not his love.

Alex wiped her nose on her sleeve. "Enough," she said, but it wasn't. The tears kept coming.

No, Travis hadn't loved her. He'd never promised her love. Good times, yes, but no love. And no forever after. He'd made that clear and she'd said that suited her, just fine.

The only trouble was, she'd lied.

What a mess she'd made of things, losing her heart to a man who'd gone out of his way to point out that her heart was the part of her he least wanted.

Wasn't that great? She wasn't just a liar, she was also a fool. And she was alone in a house that was about as cozy as a mortuary, with a storm raging outside. The only thing lacking was some guy wearing a hockey mask with an ax clutched in his hand, pounding to get in.

Something slammed against the front door.

Alex shrieked, spilled the wine down her robe and shot off the stool.

Darkness, thick and impenetrable, swirled between the library and the entry hall.

The thing hit the door a second time.

"A branch," she babbled. "It's a branch, a branch..."

Of course it was. The storm must have sent tree limbs flying. All that wind, the lightning, the rain...

The branch beat against the door again—except, this branch sounded like a fist. Alex looked around frantically for something to use as a weapon. The wine bottle? The flashlight?

The fist hit again. Alex mumbled a silent prayer and made her way to the door, bottle in one hand, flashlight in the other.

"Open this damned door, Alex!"

Alex froze. "Travis?"

"You're damned right, it's Travis. Open this door or I'll break it down."

For one crazy second, her heart filled with hope. He'd come after her. He'd come for her...

Of course he'd come for her. Women didn't just walk out on the great Travis Baron. He did the walking, the arrogant, insufferable, self-centered—

"Alex, I know you're in there. And I'm telling you right now, open—this—door!"

Alex glared at the door. He wouldn't be breaking in, not this time. She'd thrown the bolt.

"Go away, Travis," she said.

"I am not going anywhere. And I am not going to stand out here and drown while we carry on a conversation." The door rattled as he pounded his fist against it. "Alex? Do you hear me?"

Alex lifted her chin. "No."

Outside, soaked to the skin by the storm, Travis groaned

and rested his forehead against the sodden wood of the massive door.

"Alex." Travis beat his fist against the door and kicked it, too, for good measure. "Alex, I'm warning you, don't play around with me!"

She'd better not, he thought grimly. He was in a foul mood and had been, for quite a while.

The weather reports had warned of a massive storm building. Small planes had been touching down at the airstrip like bees hurrying home to the hive but he'd taken the Comanche up anyway.

"Flight's gonna be a rough one," some old geezer had warned him when he'd filed his flight plan.

A brilliant deduction, Travis had thought. But nothing would have stopped him from flying north and, by God, he'd made it, only to waste time scrounging around for a car because, by the time he landed, the rental places and the dealers were all closed. In the end, he'd paid some kid at the airfield a hundred bucks for the use of a pickup truck that smelled vaguely like horse.

What had kept him going was imagining Alex's face when she saw him. Surely, by then, she'd have come to her senses. She'd throw herself into his arms, tell him how she loved him...

Travis glowered at the closed door.

Instead, he was standing in the rain, soaked to the skin, pleading with the woman he was damned fool enough to want to spend the rest of his life with, to open the door and let him in. He had to be nuts! Here he was, putting his head in a noose. A silken noose but hey, a noose was a noose. The realization terrified him but he'd kept on going because he loved Alex. Really loved her, with the kind of chorus-singing-in-the-background, flowers-strewn-up-the aisle accompaniment he'd never believed in before.

The thing of it was, he *wanted* his head in that noose.

On the other hand, how much love could a man offer a woman if he ended up dying of pneumonia?

"Open the door, Alex."

"No."

A muscle knotted in Travis's jaw. "Alex?" he said sweetly. "Did you know you left the top down on your convertible?"

The door swung open. Travis grinned in triumph and stepped into the house as Alex stuck her head outside.

"Liar," she said furiously, and swung at him with the wine bottle. "You get out of here, Cowboy!"

Travis snatched the bottle from her, frowned and took a sniff of the air.

"Have you been drinking?"

Color flew into her face. "No. And if I have, it's none of your business, you—you liar!"

"You already called me that." He put the bottle down, slapped his hands on his hips, kicked the door closed and glared at her. Rain dripped from the tip of his nose, pooled on the floor from his sodden clothes. "And I know I lied but it was only to save my life. I was drowning out there." He put his hand up. "Will you get that light out of my eyes?"

Alex swung the light away and he got his first clear look at her. She was wearing an oversize robe with a big brown stain down the front. Her hair hung straight as sticks around her face, her eyes and nose were pink.

His heart swelled. She was beautiful.

"You can come in," she said coldly, "but only until the storm is over. I wouldn't want to have to try to explain why I'd let a man drown on the front steps."

"Thanks," he said, and shuffled past her.

"You're dripping on the floor."

"An astute observance, Princess. I don't suppose you have a towel to spare?"

She hesitated, shrugged and turned on her heel. Travis followed after her in waterlogged silence, up the stairs, down the hall, to the bedroom. A moment later, she slapped a stack of scratchy towels in his arms.

"Here."

"Thank you."

"You're welcome."

His brows lifted. "Such good manners."

"There's no reason not to be polite," she said stiffly.

He looked at the bed, then at her. "We weren't always so well mannered, when we shared a bedroom."

Alex flushed. "When you're done drying off," she said, making for the door, "come downstairs."

"I want you to come back."

Damn, he hadn't meant to tell her that way. He'd intended to take her in his arms, kiss her, tell her how she'd changed his life...but he could feel his chances slipping away. He'd never seen his Princess so cold and removed.

"Alex? I said—"

"I heard what you said." She stood absolutely still, her back to him. "What do you expect me to say, Travis?"

"That you will," he said, as if this were all too simple to need explanation.

Her heart, her foolish, foolish heart, which had been oh, so close to melting, quickly began icing over.

"Come back to you, you mean." She swung toward him.

"Yes."

He took a step forward, wishing he could see her eyes but she was pointing the flashlight at him again. His heart gave an unsteady lurch. This wasn't going right. He'd admitted that he loved her, asked her not to leave him. Why wasn't she in his arms? He knew that she loved him. She *had* to love him.

"No."

Travis came to a dead stop. "What do you mean, no?"

Alex licked her lips. Don't look at me that way, she thought. As if you really love me, not just want me. Don't, oh don't.

"Princess." He cleared his throat. "Princess, I know I let you down—"

"Is that what you think this is all about?"

"Okay. I hurt you. But I never intended to. When I said you were—that you were more than a mistress to me, I meant that you'd become the center of my life."

"That's nice," she said politely.

Travis's eyes narrowed. What was this? He was putting his heart on the line here and all she could say was...

"Nice? I bare my soul, and you tell me, 'That's nice'?"

"I am not coming back to you," she said. Her voice quavered; she told herself not to dare cry. "I hate you, Travis. I hate you!"

"No, you don't."

"Go away. And never come back."

"You're in love with me, Princess."

"In love with...?" She laughed, or hoped the sound she made was a laugh. "Oh, that ego of yours is unbelievable! Why would you think I'm in love with—" The lights blazed on. Alex blinked and looked at Travis. What she saw in his face made her breath catch. "You stay away from me, Cowboy," she said quickly, but it was too late. He was already moving toward her. She took a step back, then another. Her shoulders hit the wall.

"Don't you dare touch me, Travis! Travis? What do you think you're doing?"

"Undressing you," he said calmly.

"No!" She wriggled. A big mistake. She knew that as soon as the center of her body connected with the center of his. "Travis. Listen to me. First you broke into my house—"

"I didn't break in. And it isn't your house." He frowned. She'd never been a Girl Scout; he could tell that by the impossible knot she'd tied in the sash of her robe. "You let me in, remember?"

"Only because I didn't want your dead body on my conscience. Dammit, this won't solve anything."

"Yeah, it will." He looked up and gave her that quick, smug smile that had always managed to drive her wild. "You won't be able to lie to me, once we've made love."

"We are not going to make love!" She slapped at his hands. "Stop that!"

"Remind me to give you lessons on how to tie a square knot."

"You're never going to give me lessons in anything again."

"I am," he said calmly. "I like to sail, and I'd never let you tie a knot like this in a line on... Ah. There we are. It's open."

"I don't like boats. I am never going to sail with you..." Alex's breath caught. "Don't—don't do that."

"Do what?" he said, very softly, and he lowered his head to hers and kissed her.

"Travis," she whispered, as he stroked his hand down her throat. "Please. Please..."

He kissed her again. Her lips clung to his.

"Tell me that you love me," he said softly.

"I don't. I..." She moaned as he nuzzled her robe from her shoulder, then kissed the slope of her breast.

"Say it, Princess," he whispered.

Alex swallowed dryly. "This is coercion. It isn't fair."

Travis smiled. "You're right, it isn't." He lifted her into his arms and kissed her tenderly, again and again. "Say it anyway."

Tears stung her eyes. "All right. I admit it, I love you. I've always loved you, from the beginning."

Travis leaned his forehead against hers. "Thank you, Princess."

The tears came, then, slipping down her cheeks. "You're my soul," she whispered. "My heart. You're all I ever wanted."

"Alex. Sweet Alex." Gently, he lowered her to the bed and came down beside her. "I love you. I adore you. I don't ever want to wake in the morning without you in my arms, or go to bed without your kiss at night."

"Oh, Travis," she said in a broken whisper, "if only you really meant that..."

He drew back, trying his best to look offended. "I do mean it. When I slip a wedding ring on your finger, darlin', you'd better understand that we're goin' to be makin' those vows for all time."

Alex stared up at him. "Wedding ring? Vows? Travis… Are you asking me to marry you?"

"I'm not askin' you, Princess. I'm tellin' you. You are goin' to marry me."

Lord, he was nervous! He took a deep breath and told himself to take it easy. He wanted her to know what she was agreeing to because once she did, he'd hold her to her promise for the rest of their lives.

"Alexandra. Marry me. And be my love, forever."

Alex laughed with joy. She curled her arms around his neck and kissed him. "Yes," she whispered, between kisses. "Yes, yes…"

Travis grinned. He sat up, pulled his wet T-shirt over his head, kicked off his sneakers, rid himself of his jeans and briefs, and took her in his arms again.

"I kind of figured I'd find you here," he said.

She sighed. "Well, I had nowhere else to go. You were right, I hated Thorpe House. And I couldn't go back to your place."

"You came here because of us, darlin'. Because this is where our lives together really started."

She smiled. "You're right."

"You know, Princess, I was thinking that this place shouldn't be owned by a faceless corporation." He gave her a long, lingering kiss. "We could live here. Weekends, anyway, while we build Peregrine into what it should be."

Her face lit, and then she sighed again. "It's too late, Travis. Remember? I sold the vineyard to your father."

"Not quite. The deal didn't go through yet."

Alex smiled. "In that case, I'll call my lawyers, tell them I want to give Peregrine to you, as a wedding gift."

"You can't." That smug smile flashed across his handsome face again. "I phoned your lawyers from my plane. I bought the place for us."

"Bought it? Travis Baron, you are the most arrogant man in the world. How could you be so certain you knew what I'd say?"

"I just knew," he said, without any arrogance at all, "that neither of us could ever be whole, without the other."

The words seemed to shimmer in the air between them. "Oh, Travis," Alex whispered, and she began to weep.

Travis sighed and drew her closer. "My sister once told me I'd never be able to make sense out of women," he muttered.

"Your sister was right." Alex said, sniffling against his shoulder. "When do I get to meet her?"

"Soon," Travis said. "Very soon. But first…" He kissed her, and rose above her. "It's rainin' out, darlin'." His voice was a teasing whisper. "And you said you always wanted to take a walk in the rain."

Alex drew his head down to hers. "Later."

And, in a tumble of silken sheets and soft sighs, Travis Baron and Alexandra Thorpe came together as if for the very first time, not only in passion but in love.

Coming Next Month

HARLEQUIN PRESENTS®

THE BEST HAS JUST GOTTEN BETTER!

**#2049 MISTRESS BY ARRANGEMENT Helen Bianchin
(Presents Passion)**
Michelle is stunned when wealthy businessman
Nikos Alessandros asks her to be his social companion for a
few weeks. Will Michelle, under pressure from her family to
make a suitable marriage, find herself becoming a mistress
by arrangement?

**#2050 HAVING LEO'S CHILD Emma Darcy
(Expecting!)**
Leo insisted she marry him for the sake of their unborn child.
But despite his fiery kisses, Teri couldn't forget that Leo had
never considered marrying her before she got pregnant.
Could they turn great sex into eternal love?

**#2051 TO BE A BRIDEGROOM Carole Mortimer
(Bachelor Brothers)**
Jordan is the youngest Hunter brother. His devilish good
looks have helped him seduce any woman he's ever wanted—
except Stazy. There's only one way for Jordan to get to the
head of Stazy's queue—become a bridegroom!

#2052 A HUSBAND OF CONVENIENCE Jacqueline Baird
When an accident left Josie with amnesia, she assumed that
her gorgeous husband, Conan, was the father of her unborn
baby. They shared passionate nights until she remembered
that theirs was actually a marriage of convenience....

#2053 WEDDING-NIGHT BABY Kim Lawrence
Georgina decided she couldn't attend her ex-fiancé's wedding alone—she needed an escort! Callum Stewart was
perfect: gorgeous, dynamic...and on the night of the
wedding he became the father of her child!

**#2054 THE IMPATIENT GROOM Sara Wood
(Society Weddings)**
Prince Rozzano di Barsini whisked Sophia Charlton away to
Venice in his private jet. One whirlwind seduction later, she'd
agreed to be his bride. But why was Rozzano in such a hurry
to marry? Because he needed an heir...?